Land of Enchanters
Egyptian Short Stories from the Earliest Times to the Present Day

LAND OF ENCHANTERS

Egyptian Short Stories from the Earliest Times to the Present Day

Edited and Introduced by

Bernard Lewis and Stanley Burstein

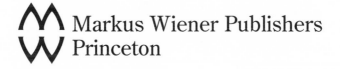 Markus Wiener Publishers
Princeton

First Markus Wiener Publishers edition, 2001

Updated and enlarged edition.
Copyright © 2001 by Bernard Lewis
First published in 1948 by The Harvill Press Ltd.

For information write to:
Markus Wiener Publishers
231 Nassau Street, Princeton, NJ 08542

Book Design by Cheryl Mirkin, CMF Graphic Design
Cover Design by Maria Madonna Davidoff
Copy-edited by Susan Lorand

Library of Congress Cataloging-in-Publication Data

Land of enchanters: Egyptian short stories from the earliest times to the present day/edited and introduced by Bernard Lewis and Stanley Burstein.
"Second Edition"—Pref.
ISBN 1-55876-266-3 (HC)
ISBN 1-55876-267-1 (PBK)
1. Short Stories, Egyptian—Translations into English.
2. Tales—Egypt. I. Lewis, Bernard. II. Burstein, Stanley Mayer.
PJ1949.L47 2001
893'.130108—DC21 2001025851

Markus Wiener Publishers books are printed in the United States of America on acid-free paper, and meet the guidelines for permanence and durability of the Committee on Production Guidelines for Book Longevity of the Council on Library Resources

Contents

The stories in Parts I, II, and III are translated and introduced by Battiscombe Gunn, unless otherwise credited.

Stanley Burstein has revised the introductions to *The Island of the Serpent, The Adventures of Sinuhe, The Tale of the Two Brothers,* and the two stories from the Coptic about Saint Pisentius.

Herodotus' *Rhampsinitus and the Clever Thief* appears in a translation by George Rawlinson revised and introduced by Stanley Burstein.

The Miracles of Khonsu is translated by Miriam Lichtheim and introduced by Stanley Burstein.

The Dream of Nectanebo is translated and introduced by Stanley Burstein.

The stories in Part IV are translated and introduced by Bernard Lewis, unless otherwise credited.

Miraculous Stories of the Pyramids and *Of Queen Charoba of Egypt and Gebirus the Metapheguian* are translated by F. Davis of Kidwelly.

The Three Walis is translated by E.W. Lane.

Naguib Mahfouz's *The Lawsuit* and *Half a Day* are translated by Denys Johnson-Davies.

Preface to the First Edition

In these pages the reader will find a selection of Egyptian short stories, dealing with many themes and ranging in time from the Middle Kingdom of Ancient Egypt to the present day. Though all from one country, the stories come from the several different civilizations that flourished there, and are translated from Middle Egyptian, Late Egyptian, Demotic, Greek, Coptic, and classical, colloquial and modern literary Arabic. Professor Battiscombe Gunn, of the University of Oxford, has made new translations of all the ancient Egyptian and Coptic stories. With the exception of two stories in a seventeenth-century English version and an anecdote from Lane's Arabian Nights, I have myself translated the Arabic stories, as far as I know, for the first time into English. I should like to take this opportunity of thanking Professor Gunn and also our Egyptian illustrator, Mr. A.S. Ali Nur, for allowing me to benefit from their advice and criticism, as well as their direct contributions.

My thanks are also due to Mahmud Taimur Bey, for permission to translate and publish his story 'Amm Mitwalli.

Bernard Lewis

Preface to the Second Edition

The publication of a new edition of this book, out of print for more than half a century, is due to the initiative of Markus Wiener, and was made possible by the scholarly collaboration of Professor Stanley Burstein. Professor Battiscombe Gunn, who was responsible for the ancient Egyptian and Coptic sections of the book, is no longer living, but Prof. Burstein has made the necessary revisions and additions in the relevant parts of the introduction and of the collection. My own contribution to this new edition consists of some correction and re-writing in those pages of the introduction dealing with the Arab and Islamic period, and some, mostly minor, corrections and revisions in the corresponding text. I would like to express my thanks and appreciation to Prof. Burstein for making this volume possible.

Bernard Lewis

Foreword

The publication of the first edition of *Land of Enchanters* was a milestone in the study of Egyptian literature. For the first time English readers could explore the full range of Egyptian short fiction from its ancient beginnings to the present. They also could do so in accurate and fluent translations that reflected the best in contemporary linguistic scholarship. This was particularly true of the translations of the ancient Egyptian texts in the volume.

Other anthologies of translations of ancient Egyptian literature had been published prior to *Land of Enchanters*, but they had been marred by their authors' decision to translate these fascinating texts into a pseudo-Archaic English modeled on the style of the King James Bible, making it difficult if not impossible to appreciate the literary qualities of the stories. Battiscombe Gunn, who was responsible for the ancient Egyptian and Coptic sections of *Land of Enchanters*, decisively broke with this tradition and produced the first modern translations of ancient Egyptian literary texts. Gunn was ideally suited to make this breakthrough. One of the most distinguished English Egyptologists of the first half of the twentieth century, Gunn had wide experience in Egyptian archaeology and possessed an unparalleled knowledge of the grammar and syntax of the various stages of ancient Egyptian, from the earliest hieroglyphic texts to Coptic, based on an exhaustive knowledge of virtually the whole range of known Egyptian texts. As a result he presented readers with unusually readable translations of these remarkable stories that reflected the most exacting scholarship but were couched in a fluent and colloquial English.

Updating a classic such as *Land of Enchanters* is a delicate task. My goal has been to incorporate the findings of contemporary Egyptology into the text without sacrificing the qualities that brought so much pleasure to readers of the first edition. To that end I have left Gunn's excellent translations unaltered, but I have revised the general introduction and the introductions to individual stories to reflect the great advances in our knowledge of Egyptian history and the character and the place of literature in ancient Egyptian culture that have occurred since the publication of the first edition over half a century ago. Here I would like to thank Professor Daniel Crecelius, California State University—Los Angeles, for his assistance in revising the general introduction to the book, and Professor Terry Wilfong, University of Michigan, for putting his expertise in Coptic literature at our disposal. I have also added two stories—"The Miracles of Khonsu" and "The Dream of Nectanebo"—to the collection in order to enable readers to obtain a fuller sense of the breadth and variety of literary activity in Ptolemaic and Roman Egypt. With these changes I hope *Land of Enchanters* will introduce a new generation of readers to one of the most remarkable literary traditions of antiquity and its legacy.

Stanley M. Burstein

INTRODUCTION

SEVERAL CIVILIZATIONS have risen, flourished and fallen in the valley of the Nile, each with its own religion, language, culture, institutions and style of life. Yet beneath them all a certain basic unity persisted. Nature defined Egypt well—the Valley and Delta of a single river, clearly demarcated by desert and sea. Man made that river an instrument of agriculture and a highway of transport. Whatever Pharaoh, Ptolemy, Caesar, Caliph or Sultan ruled in the palaces, the toiling masses of the peasants cultivated their irrigated fields and formed the solid base of a social pyramid. The needs and pressures of an agriculture dependent on the river and on the man-made canals and waterways held its layers in place. As new layers were added, the base sank deeper, but was not displaced. As the manner of cultivating the rich soil changed but little, so too did the social relationships to which it gave rise.

In few fields can this continuity of social life be seen more clearly through the variegated fabric of Egyptian history than in the love of tales and in the manner of telling them. The Egyptian has always loved a good story, and told it well. In the developing pattern of the Egyptian story, drawn on the broader canvas of Egyptian history, we can trace the variation and the enrichment of a few basic themes.

Old as are the written records of Egypt, it is by the spade that we have learned most of what we know of the earliest Egyptians. The plentiful flints of the deserts provided the first weapons and tools. Some six or more thousand years ago these first Egyptians made a revolution of far-reaching significance. They learned to graze cattle and to grow grain, first by utilizing the natural irrigation offered by the Nile floods, later by draining and clearing the marshes. But the Nile was also a road: small primitive boats made of bundles of papyrus linked the villages of valley and delta, and made possible the development of a distinctive culture throughout Egypt. By some 5,500 years ago agriculture and trade had developed far enough to permit and indeed demand the evolution of a single state. From the

Royal Tombs of Abydos, in Upper Egypt, we see how Menes, chief-tain of a clan which had the falcon as its totem, welded the valley and delta into a single realm, known as the Old Kingdom of Egypt, which he ruled as his own domain.

During the first half of the third millennium B.C.E. the pharaohs of the Old Kingdom drained swamps, extended irrigation, built towns and organized foreign trade, by land and sea, to bring Egypt the tim-ber, minerals and luxury goods she needed. But perhaps the most significant achievement of the Old Kingdom was the transformation of writing from its simple predynastic origins into an efficient and flexible tool for the expression of ideas. The catalyst for this revolu-tionary development was the growth of temple and palace stores and of a powerful central government ruling through a public administration which necessitated a system of accounts and records, and fostered the development of a new social class of clerks and scribes and the revolutionary possibility of recording, accumu-lating and transmitting knowledge in written form.

After about 2300 B.C.E. the Old Kingdom broke up, and an inter-regnum of disorder and anarchy known as the First Intermediate Period followed, during which political authority was divided among a series of rival local rulers. Economic life continued despite the absence of the strong, centralized state, and laid the foundations for the eventual reunification of the country. At the beginning of the second millennium B.C.E., the political unity of Egypt was restored by Mentuhotep II (2000–1970 B.C.E.), who ended the disorders of the preceding period and established the Middle Kingdom, a strong monarchy dominated by the former nomarchs of Thebes. The Middle Kingdom, though it lasted but two centuries, marks one of the peak points in the cultural development of ancient Egypt. With the end of the Twelfth Dynasty, however, the hold of the central gov-ernment on Egypt gradually weakened until it was overthrown by the Hyksos, an alliance of peoples from the Syro-Palestinian area, who invaded Egypt around 1730 B.C.E. and established a temporary kingdom centered in the Delta.

As early as the Old Kingdom, Egyptians realized at least some of the limitless possibilities of the new art of writing. Later Egyptian tradition credited famous figures of the Old Kingdom with various mathematical, scientific and wisdom texts. Although such early dates for these texts are now doubted, the vigorous poetic passages contained in religious works such as the Pyramid Texts and the vivid and complex narratives found in tomb autobiographies such as those of the nomarchs of Assuan attest to the growing confidence and skill with which Old Kingdom scribes used the new medium of writing. Scribal skills developed further in the interregnum that followed the collapse of the Old Kingdom, and under the pharaohs of the Middle Kingdom reached a degree of precision and sophistication that made texts written during that period classical models of language and style for many centuries.

Middle Kingdom literature reflected the tastes and values of a new official class for whom scribal training was the essential first step on the career ladder. The age-old love of a good story combined with the didactic need for "mirrors for officials"—exemplary models of the behavior of successful and righteous officials—resulted in a proliferation of fictional narratives. The most complex and popular of these works, judging by the number of surviving manuscripts, is the story of Sinuhe. Through the artful use of fictional examples of standard scribal texts—tomb autobiographies, royal letters, and royal hymns—the author of this sophisticated masterpiece of story-telling gave verisimilitude to the dramatic story of the struggle of a court official caught in the turbulence of a dynastic crisis to maintain his loyalty to his king. Similarly, the author of the stories of the Tales of a Magician showed that not even Pharaoh could pervert the values of *ma'at* (justice) that infused scribal ideals. In this—as indeed in the very creation of the short story as a literary form—the scribes of ancient Egypt broke new ground, not only for Egypt, but also for the world.

Towards the middle of the second millennium, Ahmose, ruler of Upper Egypt, succeeded in expelling the Hyksos and reestablishing a centralized monarchy which historians call the New Kingdom. He and his successors embarked on a career of imperial expansion in Asia and Africa that created an empire extending from the central Sudan to southern Syria. Imperial expansion was accompanied by prosperity in Egypt and the growth of a large and influential middle class of royal scribes, military officers, and especially priests of the Theban god Amon, whose wealth and influence threatened the traditional preeminence of the divine king. Amenhotep IV, better known as Akhenaton (ca. 1353–1336 B.C.E.), attempted to restore the king to the position of unrivaled influence and power he had enjoyed in the Old Kingdom through a religious reformation, based on the sole worship of the living sun (the Aton) and his royal avatars Akhenaton and his beautiful wife Nefertiti. Though the attempt failed, it left its mark in the rise of a new art and literature. The classical language and style of the Middle Kingdom, hitherto regarded as the sole medium for literature, was abandoned, and a vigorous literature appeared written in the vernacular language of the New Kingdom. By the end of the New Kingdom almost all the characteristic modes of Egyptian storytelling were represented in literary form—the folktale, the traveler's tale of fantasy and adventure by land or sea, the story of heroism and war, and above all the tale of wonder and witchcraft. During the centuries that followed, these forms and themes were to be adapted, remodeled, added to, enriched, and embellished, but not fundamentally changed.

Despite many political and economic crises and changes, the Bronze Age civilization of the New Kingdom survived in its essentials until the early twelfth century B.C.E., when Egypt and the other civilizations of the eastern Mediterranean entered a period of severe upheaval marked by the major migrations of peoples throughout the region known as the invasion of the Sea Peoples. Ramses III (1186–1155 B.C.E.) succeeded for a while in holding the invaders at bay, but under his successors the ancient empire of the pharaohs began to disintegrate. By the beginning of the eleventh century B.C.E., however, Egypt had lost its empire in Asia and much of its African empire a century later. During the early first millennium B.C.E. a weakened Egypt fell under the rule of Libyan, Nubian and Ethiopian dynasties, until in the early 660s B.C.E. the country was absorbed into the expanding Assyrian Empire. Although the brief Assyrian domination was followed by renewed strength and a cultural renaissance under the leadership of a new dynasty from the city of Sais, the Egyptian independence proved transitory. After a century or so of revival that saw Egyptian politics and culture influence even the new Greek cities of the Aegean, the country fell victim first to expansion of the Achaemenid Empire of Persia in 525 B.C.E., and then to the Macedonian forces of Alexander the Great in 332 B.C.E.

Egyptian civilization, and with it Egyptian storytelling, continued to flourish throughout the long period of political turmoil between the end of the Bronze Age and the Macedonian conquest. Like Middle Egyptian and Middle Kingdom literature, Late Egyptian language and literature acquired classical status, serving as models for literary composition for over half a millennium, while from Saite times onward a new and more cursive style of writing, the so-called Demotic, gradually supplanted for current usage the "hieratic" script which had been in use since the Old Kingdom. In the Hellenistic Empire of the Ptolemies, which ruled Egypt from the death of Alexander until the Roman conquest, writers began to use it for literature also, thereby once again bringing the literary language closer to vernacular speech. The result was a new golden age of narrative fiction, only fragments of which survive today.

The extensive Demotic literature, which grew up in Ptolemaic Egypt, drew on both Egyptian tradition and the literature of Egypt's ruling Greek minority, exploring new themes and even influencing Greek literature through translations such as that of the Dream of Nectanebo. Among the most famous and influential of its creations was the *Alexander Romance*, which was first written in Greek and then later translated or adapted into countless languages, becoming for over a thousand years the most widely read secular work in Eurasia.

This remarkable final flowering of Egyptian literature ended in the early centuries of the current era as the conversion of the Egyptians to Christianity and the steadily growing influence of Greek literature and thought resulted in the appearance of a new form of Egyptian, Coptic, which was written in a form of the Greek alphabet and by the fifth century C.E. had supplanted Demotic and become the literary language of Christian Egypt under late Roman and then Islamic rule. The literature of Coptic is largely a Church literature, consisting mostly of translations of scriptural and patristic texts and, in its original portions, of homilies, lives and miracles of the saints and such-like. It is remarkable that even in this literature, born of the impact on Egypt of two foreign cultures—Christianity and Hellenism—so much that is authentically Egyptian is discernible. The Coptic saints who visit Heaven and Hell and converse with mummies in tombs mark the intermediate stage between Prince Khamwise of the Demotic papyri and the sorcerers and heroes of *The Thousand and One Nights*.

The Arab invasion at the beginning of the seventh century C.E. once again brought a new language, religion and culture to Egypt. Within the short space of two years, the Muslim invaders from Arabia wrested the country from the late Roman Empire, and Egypt became a province of the Islamic Caliphate, ruled by a Governor resident in the newly established Arab garrison city of Fustat, hard by the present site of Cairo.

At first the new regime affected only the surface of Egyptian life. The old Roman civil service continued to function, collecting the old taxes in the old way, and paying them to the new masters. But gradually far-reaching changes began to take place. The creation of a new, militant Muslim Empire in the Near East, at war with the Christian Roman Empire and the new Germanic kingdoms of Europe, weakened the economic and cultural unity of the Mediterranean, which the long peace of Roman rule had established and maintained. As a result, Egypt became more and more firmly integrated into the new social and economic order being created in the lands beyond her eastern frontier, and this in turn led her to draw her cultural inspiration from Arabism and Islam rather than from Greece, Rome and Christianity.

By the second century of Muslim rule, an Arab imperial administration, using Arabic as its language and applying Muslim principles of government, had replaced that inherited from the Romans, and Arabic made steady progress as the language of government, commerce, society and culture. The rapid advance of Islam among the Egyptians, already religiously isolated from the west by their adherence to the separate Coptic Church, helped the spread of Arabic, as did also the mass settlement of Arab tribesmen from Arabia in Egypt. By the tenth century C.E. Arabic was the chief language of Egypt. Even those Egyptians who remained faithful to the older religion were using Arabic more and more in place of Coptic, whose use was increasingly becoming limited to religious purposes.

Egypt was too rich and advanced a country to remain for long a subject province of the eastern Caliphs. In the latter half of the ninth century an autonomous Muslim dynasty was established, and, except for a few brief intervals, Egypt remained an independent center of Muslim power until its absorption into the Ottoman Empire in 1517.

The most remarkable of the dynasties of mediaeval Egypt was that of the Ismaili Fatimid caliphs, who, with their newly founded city of Cairo as capital, ruled a vast empire, and vied with the Abbasid caliphs of Baghdad for the leadership of the Islamic world. But they too, like their rivals, ceased to be effective rulers and from the twelfth century onwards Egypt fell under the control of Kurdish and Turkish Mamluk dynasties. As a military quasi-feudal system based on serf agriculture replaced the freer mercantile economy of Fatimid times, the country entered a period of increasing internal weakness. The Ottoman conquest of 1517 extinguished the independent Egyptian political center, and an Ottoman Pasha was superimposed on the Mamluk feudal order. Though at times ambitious or gifted governors succeeded in restoring a measure of political autonomy, the decline in economic and cultural life continued—and was accentuated by the growing competition the new open-sea routes offered to the old Red Sea route to the East—until the invasion of Bonaparte's army confronted Egypt, for the first time since the Crusades, with the armed challenge of a militant and expanding Europe.

During the long period between the arrival of the Arabs and that of the French, the dominant cultural influence in Egypt was Arab and Islamic. Its directive impulses came from Mecca and Medina, Damascus and Baghdad, until Cairo too, under the Fatimids, became a center of Arabic culture and acquired an intellectual prominence in the Arabic-speaking world which it has retained ever since. But this Arabo-Islamic civilization was not brought ready-made by the invaders from the Arabian wilderness. Rather, it grew during the early centuries of Arab rule, incorporating and redirecting many streams of culture from earlier sources: philosophy and science from Greece, prophecy, revelation and theology from Judaism and Christianity, the theory and practice of government from Persia and Rome, arts and crafts, society and institutions from the ancient civilizations of Egypt, Syria and Mesopotamia.

These contributions from previous cultures are least noticeable in belles lettres and in poetry. Well-versed in Aristotle, Galen and Ptolemy, the Arabs knew nothing of Homer, Herodotus or the Greek dramatists, and for long preferred, even in the civilized and cosmopolitan centers of the conquered empire, to draw their literary traditions from pagan Arabia and to adhere, by and large, to the themes and techniques of pre-Islamic and early Islamic writing.

Some changes, however, were inevitable. The old stock was in the course of time developed to meet the needs of an expanding and advancing society, and modified by elements derived from the personal backgrounds of the Arabized non-Arabs who formed an ever-increasing proportion of the creators of Arabic literature. Among these, Egyptians played an important part and, as Arabic culture took firm root in Egyptian soil, they began to give it a distinctively Egyptian character, enriched by Egyptian folklore and tradition and reflecting the conditions of Egyptian life and society.

One of the most notable Egyptian contributions to the Arabic stock was in the art of the story. The native Arabic tradition was poor in narrative literature, excelling instead in the anecdote. The difficult life of the harsh Arabian desert formed a people of intense realism—and myth. The rise of Islam discouraged the borrowing of myths and legends from other nations, most of them connected with pagan deities, and, by the injunction against the pictorial representation of the human form, circumscribed the fine arts and cut off another possible inspiration of narrative literature. Even the Bedouin romances of love and war, topics dear to the Arab heart, did not achieve their full literary development in narrative form, as opposed to poetic, until they passed, along with the Arabic language, to other peoples.

Narrative literature in Arabic dates back to early times. Some stories are indigenous, such as the narrative passages in certain religious texts and the heroic tales deriving from or attributed to pre-Islamic Arabia. Others are adapted from foreign sources. An early example is the collection of animal fables known as *Kalila wa-Dimna*, translated at the beginning of the second century of Islam from a Middle Persian version of an Indian original. Another notable borrowing may be seen in the framework story and the oldest strata of *The Thousand and One Nights*.

From quite an early date Arab literary historians describe their narrative literature in some detail, and identify a number of different types of story. These include the fable or apologue; the legendary or mythic narrative; the humorous anecdote; the "evening chat"; the fantastic or even absurd tale; and, of course, the tale of heroic deeds. These stories met a growing taste in court circles, and were followed by other stories and collections from similar sources. In Egypt also the resources of the pre-Islamic past were drawn upon. Though the true history of ancient Egypt was long since lost and forgotten, the many relics still existing of a glorious past could not fail to awaken interest and curiosity, and Egyptian Arabic historians and authors began to regale their readers with a series of strange tales and miraculous narratives of a mythical past, probably derived from Coptic tradition and literature. Soon the more recent Islamic heritage was exploited in the same way and incidents in the lives of the great men of Islam as well as the legendary heroes of pre-Islamic Arabia provided the material for a gradual development from anecdote to story.

This process is particularly noticeable in Egypt, where the old and widespread taste for a good story produced many collections of anecdotes and tales ostensibly intended to point an ethical or religious moral. With the spread of the Arabic language and background, among the masses, a vast semi-popular literature appeared, in which the history and legends of Arabia and Islam were worked into connected romances in interspersed prose and verse, suitable for public recitation.

Perhaps the best and certainly the most popular was the romance of 'Antar, a long and loosely constructed tale of love, war and honor, recounting the innumerable adventures of one of the most famous of ancient Arab heroes. The migration of the Hilali tribes from Arabia to Egypt and from Egypt to North Africa in the eleventh century provided the theme for another cycle, while the career of Baybars, the thirteenth-century Mamluk sultan of Egypt who defeated both the Crusaders and the Mongols, was worked into a heroic romance.

Of a rather different character is the famous collection of *The Thousand and One Nights*. Of Persian and perhaps Indian origin, this collection was translated into Arabic at an early date, and augmented by new tales born in Islam, many of which are of Egyptian origin, faithfully reflecting the different aspects of Egyptian taste. Besides a number of tales of Arab chivalry and war, there are many of a more urban type, describing the life of the merchants and artisans of the Egyptian cities, often with remarkable realism and vigor that bespeak a mature town civilization. Related to these are the picaresque tales, stories of ingenious roguery by city sharpers and thieves, usually with ironic reflections on the honesty and efficiency of the police. Tales of this kind have long enjoyed particular popularity in Egypt, and examples range from the amusing Egyptian legend of the clever thief retailed by Herodotus to innumerable contemporary anecdotes and folktales. Many collections of adventures of this type, some of them attributed to heroes of *The Thousand and One Nights*, were current in Mamluk and Ottoman Egypt.

Another distinctively Egyptian contribution to *The Thousand and One Nights* and other Arabic collections is the tale of fantasy. From the earliest times, when the Neolithic barbarians of the Nile Valley showed by the elaborateness of their burial grounds their growing interest in a life beyond this life, and an unusually powerful priesthood strengthened its grip on the minds and purses of the people by dispensing its vaunted power to control the judges and judgments of the unseen world, Egyptians have been fascinated by the miraculous and the supernatural, and have reveled in tales of wonder and enchantment. To the common Arabic pool they contributed count-less stories of magicians and ogres, of witchcraft and supernatural beings. The Egyptians, if foremost, are by no means alone among the Near Eastern peoples in their taste for the supernatural. While the pre-Islamic Arab poets sometimes spoke of ghouls and other beings, and the legend world of Persia is peopled by divs and peris as well as human beings, scholars have noticed a significant differ-ence between the Egyptian and the other spirits. While the Arabian ghouls are no more than personifications of the mysterious loneli-ness of the desert by night, and the Persian divs and peris—Islamized into 'ifrits and jinn in the Arabic versions—are active per-sonalities with an independent role and character of their own, working for or against the hero according to temperament and incli-nation, the spirits of Egyptian story are often the passive slaves of some talisman, charm or place, bound to obey the command and serve the purpose of its master, incapable of any will or action but the blind fulfillment of their allotted tasks. In the words of one story, "the land of Egypt is a land of enchanters, and the Sea there is full of spirits and demons, which assist them to carry on their affairs."

All these semi-popular romances and tales form an intermediate stage between the formal classical literature in correct literary Arabic and the folklore of the illiterate peasants. In language they range from almost pure classical Arabic to something approaching the unwritten vernacular of the masses, in form from the carefully constructed short story to the rambling romances of the coffee-house reciters. Below them in the literary hierarchy comes the folk-tale proper—the popular story of the Egyptian villages, handed down by word of mouth only and little influenced by the foreign streams of culture that have entered into the Nile Valley in the course of the centuries. It is only during the twentieth century that these stories have been recorded in their original form, initially by the efforts of European scholars, who took them down in a phonet-ic transcription as told in the teller's native dialect. Though recent in a formal sense, many of them are undoubtedly of high antiquity, and contain elements of Egyptian folklore going back to Pharaonic times.

It could hardly be otherwise. The life of the Egyptian peasant, the ultimate creator of Egyptian life and art, has varied little through the ages, and his manner of describing life or escaping from it has been stereotyped through the millennia into well-defined moulds that have found their way into the more formal literatures of the towns-folk and of the learned. The same qualities of acute observation combined with superabundant fantasy, the same mingling of naivete and subtlety, enrich the tales of the illiterate cook as those of the public reciter or the relaxing theologian.

The brief French occupation in 1798–1801 had little immediate effect on Egypt. It did, however, strengthen already existing European interest in the country, and brought Egypt into the forefront of international affairs as a battleground of rival European imperialisms and an essential link in both commercial and military communications. The new importance of the country, together with the work of the distinguished gathering of savants who accompanied General Napoleon Bonaparte on his Egyptian campaign, provided Europeans with their first detailed exposure to both the remains of ancient Egypt and contemporary Egyptian life, and helped to pave the way for the introduction of Western influence into the country.

In the first half of the nineteenth century, after a brief and tormented interlude of restored Ottoman rule, Egypt passed under the rule of an ambitious and gifted Pasha, Muhammad 'Ali, founder of the dynasty that held the throne of Egypt until 1952, when the last king, Faruq, was deposed and went into exile. Rapidly freeing himself from all but nominal Ottoman suzerainty, Muhammad 'Ali embarked on a far-reaching program of reorganization and reform, involving the creation of a new army trained and equipped on Western lines, the rationalization of agriculture, the construction of factories, the building of technical schools and hospitals, and the sending, for the first time, of student missions to Europe.

Though these reforms were primarily military in intention, their effects went far beyond military bounds. After Muhammad 'Ali's retirement in 1848, much of the momentum behind his work was lost, but his descendants and successors, recognized as hereditary governors of an autonomous tributary province, resumed the program of reform he had initiated, albeit on a smaller scale and at a slower pace. The opening of the Suez Canal in 1869 and the rapid development of European commercial and financial interests in Egypt gave a great impetus to the spread of European techniques and ideas, and the British occupation of 1882 still further accelerated the process by vastly increasing the scope of European activities and by provoking the rise of a nationalist movement, some of whose leaders saw in the adoption of Western methods an essential prerequisite to the successful pursuit of national aspirations.

One of the key figures of the cultural revival was Rifa'a Rafi' at-Tahtawi (1801–1873), a sheikh of the Azhar Mosque, who resided in Paris from 1826 to 1831 as religious preceptor to the student mission. He seems to have been far more successful in assimilating French culture than any of his wards, and played an important part in Muhammad 'Ali's school system and in his program of translations of technical, scientific and other works into Arabic. His Arabic version of Fenelon's *Télémaque* was published in 1867, and its popularity is attested by the appearance of no less than three more Arabic translations by 1912. Other translations, from various hands, followed in increasing numbers. *The Count of Monte Cristo* appeared in Arabic dress in Cairo in 1871. In the following year 'Uthman Jalal, Rifa'a's best pupil, published the first of several Arabic versions of *Paul et Virginie*, adapted to local taste. A series of novels by Victor Hugo, Jules Verne, Eugene Sue and others followed, while numerous excerpts and short stories were translated and published in the press, in anthologies, and in a growing number of periodicals devoted exclusively to this type of matter.

An important role in the dissemination of Western culture in Egypt was played by Syrian refugees from Ottoman rule, who were attracted to British-occupied Egypt by its material prosperity and its relative freedom of expression. Many of them were Christians, educated in French and American mission schools, and less inhibited by the conservative influences of their traditional culture in accepting Western ideas. From their intermediate position between the Arab and European worlds, they were able to act as guides and mentors to a new generation of Egyptian intellectuals entering the world

of Western ideas. The increase in literacy, the development of print-
ing and the growth of an extensive periodical press provided the
material opportunities for a rapid expansion, first of translations and
adaptation of European texts, and, ultimately, of original works,
while the introduction of English into the Egyptian schools broad-
ened and diversified the sources of Western inspiration.

The taste that governed the choice of texts for translations was at
first erratic. As might have been expected, the wonder stories of
Jules Verne and the adventures of Arsene Lupin and of Sherlock
Holmes found a ready welcome among the people of the Arabian
Nights. But more serious literature was not neglected, and Maupassant, Daudet and Dickens, to name but three, found translators and
disciples in Egypt.

The first attempts at original storytelling were made by Syrians,
of whom Jurji Zaidan (1861–1914), the author of twenty-odd Arab
historical romances modeled on Dumas, is the most notable. The
Egyptians soon rivaled and surpassed their Syrian teachers. More
conservative than the Syrians, the first modern Egyptian novelists
and short-story writers attempted to adapt modern material to the
classical Arabic literary forms, and notably to the *maqamat*. These,
in classical Arabic literature, were a series of loosely related incidents, described in rhymed prose, barely qualifying for the title of
short stories, and used as pegs on which the authors would hang
their verbal ingenuity and stylistic artifices. Simplified and related to
modern conditions, and used as a vehicle of social comment and
criticism, the *maqamat* of Muhammad Ibrahim al-Muwailihi (1868–
1930) and of his imitators may be regarded as the first steps towards
the creation of the modern Egyptian novel.

One of the leading figures of the Egyptian literary revival was
Mustafa Lutfi al-Manfaluti (1876–1924). Best known as a poet and
essayist of distinction, he also adapted many short stories from
French models, and wrote a number of his own, most of them sen-
timental and didactic. In the early years of the twentieth century a
group of short-story writers, led by Muhammad Taimur (1892–
1921), broke new ground in the observation and description of contemporary life, and carried the Egyptian story a long way beyond

the fumbling efforts of the first somewhat hesitant innovators.

There was much to impede the development of modernist literature in Egypt. The forces of conservatism were still strong, and even where they had lost their intellectual grip on an author's mind, they left their mark through the training and education of his early, formative years, leaving him dissatisfied with the old, yet unequipped to receive the new. The reading public, though increasing, was still small, and, moreover, those with the taste for western-style fiction preferred to read French and English books, and neglected the native product. The continued use of classical Arabic as the sole literary language made realistic dialogue difficult, while the use of the vernacular was opposed both because of its lowly status and, later, because of its potential threat to the unity of the Arabic-speaking peoples.

The formal end of Ottoman suzerainty in 1914, the movement culminating in the partial realization of political independence in 1922, and the enormous increase in the material prosperity of Egypt in the interwar years made possible a vast extension of the reading public and a corresponding development of modernism. Unlike some of their colleagues elsewhere, the Egyptian modernists attempted, not the complete abandonment of the traditional heritage, but rather a blending of the two worlds in a modernized, yet still essentially Egyptian, culture. The contradictions that underlay this project and the conflicts that arose from it enriched early-twentieth-century Egyptian literature with a multitude of themes, and resulted in the creation of an extensive and often remarkable narrative literature, contemporary in its themes and in its techniques, that was particularly successful in the short story. Certainly the most successful short-story writer in Arabic of the period was Mahmud Taimur, whose many volumes of tales revealed a steadily increasing mastery of technique and firm roots in Egyptian soil. Another Egyptian writer, the Nobel Prize winner Naguib Mahfouz, is better known for his novels, but is also the author of a number of striking short stories.

It is a long journey from the anonymous scribes of the Middle Kingdom to the Westernized novelists of present-day Cairo. Yet one can discern a pattern through the many changes of material, theme, color and style. Perhaps the most striking feature of Egyptians through all their ages is the vitality and variety of their imaginations. The shipwrecked sailor who peopled a remote isle with beasts and gods, the Coptic saint who conversed with the dead from the underworld, the Muslim hero who bent the ogress to his will, and the Cairene doorkeepers who saw in a humble hawker of peanuts and melon a wonder-working saint, are all inspired by the same rich and unbounded fantasy, the same desire to escape from the brown monotony of the Nile Valley and the ceaseless toil that it demands.

It is perhaps the same theme of escape that underlies a second characteristic of Egyptian storytelling: the love of the picaresque. Egypt is a flat, open country, easily controlled, and subjected in almost all periods by the needs of her irrigated agriculture to the rule of a single central government. This land without mountains or forests has known no Spartacus or Robin Hood, and so the resentments of the masses against heavy-handed authority, unable to embroider the exploits of popular heroes of revolt, have found their outlet instead in tales of thieves and sharpers, humble men of the cities who, by a combination of audacity and craft, have defied and outwitted the rich and the mighty amid the acclamations of the dispossessed. Both themes, the fantastic and the picaresque, have been helped in their development by the growth of foreign travel. Lacking both timber and metal, Egypt was compelled, from the very beginning of organized social life, to send merchants, envoys and sometimes soldiers to foreign lands in search of what she needed. The returning traveler is ever a source of tales of wonder and imagination. The picaresque hero, by the very nature of his avocation, is inclined to frequent changes in his sphere of action.

The fantastic is by no means the sole characteristic of Egyptian storytelling. The New Kingdom traveler Wenamun gives an accurate and factual account of the countries and peoples through which he passed, while the mediaeval Ahmad ibn Yusuf has given us a series of vignettes of everyday life of remarkable vigor and truth. Even the supernatural creatures of peasant legend are described in a dry, matter-of-fact style that makes them appear almost as normal as the human heroes themselves, and shows how the realism of some of the modernists is not entirely an importation from Europe.

Yet it is by the limitless wealth of imagination that Egyptian literature is chiefly distinguished, and it is thanks to this quality in its literature, religion and monuments that the country impressed Hebrew, Greek, Arab and Western European alike as a land of magic and wonder, the legendary "Land of Enchanters."

ANCIENT EGYPT

The Island of the Serpent

There is only one manuscript of this story, which is preserved in St. Petersburg and dates to about 1900 B.C.E. The beginning of the manuscript is lost, and with it the explanation of the circumstances causing a certain Count to be fearful about an audience he is to have with the King. The beginning of the tale suggests that it involved a voyage to Nubia. All that survives of the story, however, is a long speech addressed to the Count by a "good attendant," who attempts to encourage him by recounting a mission of his own that ended disastrously, but from which he emerged happily, having received honors from Pharaoh. The story ends with an obscure remark by the Count that suggests, however, that the "good attendant's" story has not altered his pessimistic view of the probable outcome of the upcoming audience. The story's dramatic account of shipwreck, miraculous rescue, and mysterious islands reflects the beginnings of Egyptian voyages to the wondrous land of Punt during the second millennium B.C.E. and the fabulous wealth that could be acquired there. Tales like this one may have influenced the Hellenistic Greek authors of travel romances set in the seas south of Egypt, such as Euhemerus and Iamboulus, and, more remotely, the medieval authors of the tales of Sindbad the Sailor and Sir Thomas More, whose *Utopia* marked the beginning of the modern utopian tradition.

. . . And the good attendant[1] said:

"Good news, Count! See, we have reached home! The mallet has been taken in hand and the mooring-stake driven in, the tying-up rope having been placed on land. They are giving praise, and thanking God; they are all embracing one another. Our crew has returned in good order; there is none missing from our expedition. We reached Lower Nubia, we have passed Bigah.[2] See then, we have returned in peace, we have reached our own land.

"Listen to me, Count; I am not over-talkative. Wash yourself, pour water over your fingers. Then will you answer when you are addressed, and speak to the King with presence of mind; you will answer without hesitation. A man's mouth saves him: his speech obtains indulgence for him. But do as you wish; talking to you thus wearies you.

"I will relate to you, then, something similar which happened to myself when I went to the Mine-country for the Sovereign. I went down to the sea in a ship of 120 cubits in length and 40 cubits in width,[3] in which were 120 sailors, of the best of Egypt; whether they looked at the sky or whether they looked at the land, their hearts were stouter than lions'. They foretold a storm before it had come, and foul weather before it had arisen.

"The storm broke out while we were yet on the sea, before we could make the land. The wind arose and made a great noise, with waves eight cubits[4] high. The wave even struck the mast.[5] The ship perished, and of those that were in it not one survived except me. Then I was cast on an island by a wave of the sea. I spent three days alone, with only my heart for my companion, lying within a shelter of wood, and I clung to the shade.[6]

"Then I got to my feet to find out what I could put in my mouth.

---

1. I.e. an attendant of the King; see the end of the story.
2. A small island at the southern frontier of Egypt.
3. About 206 by 70 feet.
4. 14 feet.
5. According to the interpretation of Miriam Lichtheim, *Ancient Egyptian Literature*, vol. 1: *The Old and Middle Kingdoms* (Berkeley and Los Angeles: University of California Press, 1973), p. 215 n. 1.
6. For fear of being seen?

I found figs and grapes there, and all kinds of fine vegetables; sycamore figs of two kinds were there, and cucumbers as though they were cultivated. Both fish and fowl were there; there is nothing that was not in that island. Then I ate my fill. I put food aside, because I had so much by me, and having shaped a fire-stick I kindled fire, and made a burnt-offering to the gods.

"Then I heard a thunderous noise, which I felt sure was a wave of the sea: the trees were splitting, the earth was shaking. When I uncovered my face I found that it was a serpent that was coming. He was thirty cubits long, and his beard was more than two cubits long.[7] His body was plated with gold, his eyebrows were of real lapis lazuli; he was extremely intelligent.

"He addressed me, while I was on my belly before him, and said to me, 'What has brought you, what has brought you, little one, what has brought you? If you delay in telling me what has brought you to this island, I will cause you to find yourself burnt up, having become one who cannot be seen.' He went on speaking to me but I heard it not; I was on my belly before him and had become unconscious.

"Then he placed me in his mouth and carried me off to his resting-place. He set me down, and I was unscathed; I was safe and sound, not being overpowered. He addressed me while I was on my belly before him, and said to me, "What has brought you, what has brought you, little one, what has brought you to this island of the sea, whose borders are in the waters?"

"Then I made answer to him, my arms being bent before him,[8] and said to him, 'I went down to the Mine Country, on business of the Sovereign, in a ship of 120 cubits in length and 40 cubits in width, in which were 120 sailors, of the best of Egypt; whether they looked at the sky or whether they looked at the land, their hearts were stouter than lions'. They foretold a storm before it had come, and foul weather before it had arisen. Every one of them was stouter of heart and stronger of hand than his fellow; there was no

---

7. 51-1/2 and 3-1/2 feet.
8. A deferential attitude.

fool among them. The storm broke out while we were yet on the sea, before we could make the land. The wind arose and made a great noise, with waves eight cubits high. The wave even struck the mast.[9] The ship perished, and of those that were in it not one survived except me, and here I am in your presence. I was brought to this island by a wave of the sea.'

"And he said to me, 'Do not fear, do not fear, little one, do not avert your face; you have reached me; see, God has preserved you that he might bring you to this island to please me. There is nothing that is not in it, it is full of all good things.

"'See, you will spend month upon month on this island until you have completed four months, and a ship will arrive from the Residence[9] in which will be sailors who are known to you. You will go away with them to the Residence, and you will die in your city.

"'How glad is he who relates what he has experienced, when painful things are past! Now I will relate to you something similar which happened in this island. I was in it with my kinsmen, and children were among them: we amounted to seventy-five serpents, my children and my kinsmen, without my mentioning to you the daughter whom I gained through prayer.[10] Then a star fell, and these went up in fire through it. It chanced that I was not with them; they were burnt, and I was not in their midst. Then I died for them,[11] when I found them to be a single heap of corpses.

"'But if you have enough patience you will embrace your children, you will kiss your wife, and see your house, and these things are best of all; you will reach your home in which you were, in the midst of your kinsmen.'

"Crouching on my belly I touched the ground before him [with my forehead], and then said to him, 'I will describe your might to the Sovereign, and cause him to be acquainted with your greatness. I will send you fine oils and perfumes, and the incense of the temples wherewith every god is propitiated, and I will relate what has

---

9. Namely, the city where the King and his court reside, which is not necessarily the capital of the country.

10. According to the interpretation of Lichtheim, 1:213.

11. An exaggerated expression for grief.

happened, having in mind what I have seen through his [the Sovereign's] might. Thanks shall be returned to you in the Capital, in the presence of the Council of the entire land. I will slaughter oxen for you as a burnt-offering, and wring the necks of fowl for you. And I will send you ships laden with all the luxuries of Egypt, as should be done for a god who loves men in a far country that men know not.'

"Then he laughed at me, and at this that I had said as being vanity in his opinion, and said to me, 'You have not much myrrh and every kind of incense[12] but I am the Ruler of Punt,[13] and myrrh belongs to me. And that fine oil which you said should be brought is the chief thing of this island. And it shall come about that when you depart from here, nevermore will you see this island; it will have become water.'

"That ship came, even as he had previously foretold. And I went and set myself on a high tree, and I recognized those who were in the ship. I went to announce the matter, but found that he knew it. And he said to me, 'Farewell, farewell, little one, to your house, that you may see your children. Let my repute be good in your city; see, that is all I require of you.'

"Then I cast myself on my belly before him, my arms bent. And he gave me a cargo of myrrh, fine oil, various gums, essences and perfumes, eye-paint, giraffes' tails, a great packet of incense, elephants' tusks, swift hounds, monkeys, apes, and all good and costly things. And I loaded them on to this ship. When I had cast myself on my belly to thank him, he said to me, 'See, you will reach the Residence within two months and will embrace your children and grow young again at the Residence, and be embalmed [there].'

"Then I went down to the shore, near this ship, and I called to the soldiers who were in it. I gave praise on the shore to the lord of this island, and those who were in the ship did likewise.

---

12. According to the interpretation of Lichtheim, 1:214.
13. A country on the African side of the Red Sea, most probably in the central Sudan and Eritrea, and one of the principal sources of incense and other exotic African products. Punt and its products are vividly depicted in a famous set of reliefs in the mortuary temple of Hatshepsut (1478–1458 B.C.E.) at Deir el-Bahri.

"We sailed away northwards to the Residence of the Sovereign, and we arrived at the Residence in two months, exactly as he had said. Then I entered in to the Sovereign and presented to him these gifts which I had brought from this island. And he thanked me in the presence of the Council of the entire land. Then I was made an Attendant, and was endowed with two hundred head of slaves.

"Behold me, after I had reached land, after I saw what I had experienced. Listen to my utterance. See, it is good to listen to people."

Then the Count said to him, "Do not play the virtuous man, friend. Does one give water to a bird the day before when it is going to be killed in the morning?"

It has been copied from beginning to end, according to what was found in writing. Written by the scribe with clever fingers, Amen'o (may he live, be prosperous and healthy!), son of Ameny.

The Adventures of Sinuhe

To judge by the number of the manuscripts (mostly very fragmentary) on papyrus, limestone flake, or potsherd that have come down to us—over a score—the story of Sinuhe ("Son of the Sycamore-tree") was one of the most popular of Egyptian literary texts. These manuscripts range in date from about 1800 B.C.E. (some 150 years after the events told of are said to have taken place) to about 1100 B.C.E. None of them is quite complete; the two most extensive, which complement one another, are among the oldest and textually best.

How far this narrative is an authentic autobiographical record, how far a work of imagination, are questions which have much exercised scholars. There is nothing incredible in it; and, except for its length, the whole story, especially at its beginning and end, resembles so much some inscriptions on the walls of tombs that it has been thought possible that such an inscription was the original of our text. Sinuhe's tomb was made, he tells us, at the "Residence" of the time—namely, at El-Lisht—some forty miles south of Cairo; but his burial-place has not been discovered by the excavators who have explored that site. Of himself there is no contemporary mention. But in view of the destruction of tombs, the paucity of records, and the fact that Sinuhe does not say that he played any part in affairs of state in Egypt, the absence of any solid evidence of his existence does not constitute proof that he is merely a fictitious character.[1]

Of internal evidence of the authenticity of the story there is little or none. The two kings and the queen who figure in it are, of course, historical; but nothing is known, apart from what Sinuhe tells us, of the Asiatic king Amemnenshi. Of the dozen or more places outside Egypt that are mentioned, only one—Keshu—is not attested from other sources.[2] But it has been pointed out that there is nothing in the Asiatic part of the narrative, including the description of the products of Ya'a, which could not have been thought of by a stay-at-home author knowing the names and roughly the relative positions of a certain number of places in Palestine and Syria.

Turning to the narrative content of the text, it will escape no reader that the motive which impelled Sinuhe to live away from Egypt for many years is highly obscure. The obscurity is probably intentional. It is clearly connected with the death of King Ammenemes I (who, we now know, was murdered as a result of a conspiracy) and the question of the succession. The old king's eldest son, Sesostris, who had been co-regent with him for a decade and was his natural successor, was returning from a campaign in Libya at the time— he seems to have reached a point very near, if not within, the Egyptian frontier—and was naturally informed of his father's death by messengers. On receiving this news he pushed on to the "Residence" with all possible speed. But there seems to have been a court plot (perhaps formed by the murderers of the old king) to set another of the King's sons on the throne; this prince, also returning from Libya, had been summoned for a conference, and Sinuhe heard the conversation between him and some other person or persons not specified. Hearing this conversation put Sinuhe into a state of wild panic, with a frantic desire to get out of Egypt and as far away from it as possible. But why did what he heard affect him in this way? The most obvious answer is that by overhearing state secrets of the highest importance Sinuhe had come to know far too much, and that the subversive court party, if they once knew that he was privy to their aims, though unintentionally, would be content with nothing less than his death. Sinuhe's own references to the cause of his flight are various and contradictory: he tells us in different places that (a) a god possessed him and drove him to a flight that was pre-ordained; (b) his own heart impelled him to roam abroad (a view shared by the King in his letter); (c) he simply doesn't know. In three places Sinuhe

---

1. That the sheikh who saved his life in the desert recognized him, and that Egyptians at the court of the Asiatic king were able to testify to his character and capabilities are, however, evidence that he was fairly well known in his time—according to the story.

2. The position of Keshu, also that of Ya'a, are unknown. Note also that, within Egypt, Lake Ma'ati, Nuhet, the Island of Snefru, Gar and Peten cannot be located at all closely.

or the King's children say that he fled through fear of the King; once Sinuhe says definitely that he was not afraid.[3] One of Sinuhe's commentators says that "it is not the least attractive point about this fascinating tale that its very mainspring is so elusive";[4] but others may find this elusiveness somewhat irritating, reflecting, however, that the story was not written for us, and that its Egyptian readers may have understood well the background against which this drama of high events was played. Today it seems impossible to obtain from the various statements in the narrative any clear, coherent idea of the causes of the flight.

That Sinuhe should express a strong sense of having deeply offended the King by going abroad, and utter a prayer for forgiveness and permission to return, and that this should be followed by receipt of a letter in which the King exhausts every means of persuasion to induce him to return, doubtless is not a contradiction, but shows that Sinuhe, laboring under a sense of guilt, wholly misunderstands the King's attitude towards him.

The Adventures of Sinuhe is written in a style that is more elaborate than that of any other Egyptian composition known to us. Its author employs every sentence construction and literary device known in his period together with a rich vocabulary to give variety and color to his narrative. The pleasure of the ancient reader was further enhanced by his artful use of typical scribal forms such as tomb autobiography, royal hymn, and royal letter to create a sense of versimilitude for his account of the adventures of his hero. The result is a subtle and complex masterpiece that, in the perceptive words of one critic,[5] "reassuringly presents the values of the Egyptian way of life, but the possibility of a world elsewhere lingers in the audience's mind . . . .This ambivalence is reflected in the setting of the *Tale* [*of Sinuhe*] in a tomb, which is a link between the imperfect world of men and the perfection of the otherworld."

The hereditary prince and count, treasurer of the King of northern Egypt, sole Companion,[6] provincial administrator of the domains of the Sovereign in the lands of the Bedouins, the real,

---

3. This is not the only contradiction in the story. Since the King's children were standing in the gateway of the Palace to meet Sinuhe on his return from abroad (see p. 43), why do they evince such complete surprise and indeed incredulity on being told by their father a little later that the man with him is Sinuhe?

4. Alan H. Gardiner, *Notes on the Story of Sinuhe,* p. 14; the quotation below is on p. 164.

5. R. B. Parkinson, *The Tale of Sinuhe and other Ancient Egyptian Poems 1940–1640 BC* (Oxford: Oxford University Press, 1997), pp. 25–26.

6. An honorific title for the highest class of courtiers.

beloved king's acquaintance, the attendant Sinuhe, says:

I am an attendant who follows his lord, and a servant of the Princess greatly favored in the royal Harem, wife of King Sesostris [I] in the town Khnemiswet, daughter of King Ammenemes [I] in the town Kanefru,[7] the honored lady Nefru.

In the thirtieth year of his reign,[8] the third month of the inundation season, the seventh day of the month, the god mounted to his horizon, the King of southern and northern Egypt, Sehtepyebre,[9] ascended to heaven, uniting with the sun, the divine flesh being mingled with him who made it.[10] The Residence[11] was in silence, hearts were grief-stricken, the great Double Door [of the palace] was closed, the courtiers sat with head on lap, the people mourned.

Now his Majesty had sent a military expedition to the land of the Libyans, his eldest son being in command of it, the good god, King Sesostris;[12] and he [Sesostris] was returning, having brought away captives of the Tehnu people[13] and all kinds of herds and flocks without limit. The Companions of the Court had sent to the western side[14] to inform the King's son[15] of the state of affairs that had come about in the Royal Apartments.[16] The messengers found him on the road; they reached him in the evening-time. He did not delay a moment; the Falcon[17] flew with his henchmen without letting his army know.

Now the King's sons who were under him in this army had been sent for, and one of them had been summoned.[18] Now I was standing still, and heard his voice while he was speaking afar off, while I was near [him who was addressing him]. My heart was distraught,

---

7. Khnemiswet and Kanefru are the places in which the kings in question had built their pyramids.
8. In about the year 1970 B.C.E.
9. "Throne-name" of Ammenemes I.
10. A poetical statement of King's death.
11. See, on this word, p. 26, note 9, above.
12. Sesostris I had been co-regent with his father for about ten years.
13. Inhabitants of part of the Libyan Desert, west of Egypt.
14. On the west of northern Egypt, towards Libya.
15. The eldest, Sesostris.
16. The private part of the palace, the living-rooms of the royal family.
17. The King was identified with the falcon-god Horus.
18. On all this see p. 30, above.

my hands hung open, all my members fell to trembling. I ran leaping away to find somewhere to hide myself. I placed myself between
two bushes, to sunder the road from him who was walking on it.[19]
I proceeded southwards; I did not plan to reach this[20] Residence, for
I expected that civil strife would break out, and I did not think to
live after him.[21]

I crossed Lake Ma'ati, near Nuhet, and landed at the Island of
Snefru, and spent the day on the edge of the river. I set forth when
it was day. If I met a man standing in my path, he respected me,
being afraid. When supper-time arrived, I reached the district of
Gaw, and crossed over in a barge without a rudder, by means of a
westerly breeze. I passed east of the quarry beyond the Lady of Red
Hill.[22] I continued on foot northwards and touched the Walls of the
Ruler,[23] made to repel the Bedouins and crush the Sandfarers.[24] I
took up a crouching position under a bush, in fear lest the watch for
the day on top of the wall might be looking. I went on at evening-
time; when it dawned I reached Peten, and stopped at the Island of
Kemwer,[25] for an attack of thirst had overtaken me. I was parched,
my throat was full of dust, and I thought, "This is the taste of death!"

Then I lifted up my heart, to pull myself together, for I heard the
sound of the lowing of cattle and caught sight of Bedouins. A sheikh
among them, who had been in Egypt, recognized me. Then he gave
me water, and boiled milk for me. I went with him to his tribe, and
they treated me kindly.

One country passed me on to another. I set forth from Byblos,[26]
and turned back to Kedmi,[27] where I spent half a year. Amem-nen-
shi, the king of Upper Retjenu,[28] sent for me and said to me, "You

---

19. That is, as often as he saw anyone coming he hid by the roadside.
20. Where Sinuhe is at the time of writing his memoirs.
21. The dead King.
22. A temple of Hathor. Red Hill (still so called) is a little east of Cairo.
23. Built as a barrier to protect the north-east frontier of Egypt from invasion and
infiltration.
24. A nickname for the nomads of the deserts of Sinai, Palestine and Arabia.
25. The modern Bitter Lakes, on the Isthmus of Suez.
26. About twenty miles north of Beirut, on the Syrian coast.
27. Probably the desert region east of Damascus.
28. The mountainous part of Palestine.

will be happy with me; you will hear Egyptian." He said this, knowing my character and having heard of my capacities; the Egyptians who were there with him had borne witness to me.

Then he said to me, "Why ever have you come all this way? Has anything happened at the Residence?"

And I said to him, "King Sehtepyebre has passed to the Horizon, and it is not known what may happen in consequence." But I added, dissembling, "I returned from an expedition to the land of the Libyans, and something was reported to me; my mind grew faint, my heart was no longer in my body, it brought me along desert paths. I was not criticized, no one spat in my face, I heard no insulting phrase, my name was not heard in the mouth of the reporter.[29] I do not know what brought me to this country; it is like a dispensation of God."

Then he said to me, "How shall that land do without him, that beneficent god, the fear of whom used to pervade the countries like that of Sakhmet[30] in a year of plague?"

And I said to him, answering him:

"But his son has entered the palace
and taken the heritage of his father.

And he is a god, without a rival:
No other such has existed before him.

He is a master of wisdom, perfect in plans, of beneficent
     commands:
Men move up and down [the land] according to his order.

It is he who subdued the foreign lands while his father
     was in his palace,
And reported to him when what he had ordained was done.

---

29. A military officer, who reports to higher authorities on deeds of bravery and the reverse, among other matters.

30. A terrible lioness-goddess, believed to cause plagues.

And he is a mighty man, achieving by his strength of arm:
A man of action without an equal,
Who is seen felling the barbarian host,
Throwing himself into the fray.

He is a curber of the horn,[31] a weakener of hands:
His enemies cannot draw up their forces.

He is clear-sighted, a smasher of skulls:
None can stand up near him.

He is swift-stepped to destroy the fugitive:
He who turns his back to him has no bourne.

He is high-hearted in the moment of repulse:
He is one who puts to flight, and does not turn his own back.

He is stout-hearted when he sees a host:
He does not allow sloth about his heart.

He is eager when he sees the melée:
To strike down the barbarian horde is his joy.

He takes up his shield and tramples under foot:
He does not strike twice in order to kill.

There is none who can turn aside his arrow:
None who can draw his bow.

The barbarians flee before him
As before the might of the Great One.[32]

He fights, having foreseen the end:
He spares not, and there is no remainder.

---

31. An image taken from hunting wild bulls.
32. The cobra (*uraeus*) on the king's brow, which destroys his enemies.

He is a master of charm, of great sweetness:
He has conquered by love.

His city loves him more than itself:
It rejoices in him more than in its own god.
Men and women exult in him surpassingly now that he is king.

He conquered while yet in the egg:[33]
His face having been set toward it [conquest] since his birth

He increases those who were born with him:
He is unique, of God's gift.

How does this land rejoice that he has come to rule!
He is one who widens boundaries.

He will conquer the southern countries:
He will despise the northern lands.

He has been created to strike down the Bedouins,
To crush the Sandfarers.

"Send to him, acquaint him with your name as that of an enquir-
er far from His Majesty. He will not fail to do good to a country that
is submissive to him."

And he said to me, "Why then, Egypt is happy, for she knows that
he flourishes. See, you are here, and so you shall live with me; I will
treat you well."

He placed me at the head of his children, and married me to his
eldest daughter. He let me choose for myself some of his country,
even of the best that he had on his boundary adjoining another
country. It is a good land, Ya'a by name; figs and grapes are in it; it
has more wine than water, it has much honey and olive oil in plenty; all fruits are upon its trees; limitless barley and spelt are there,

---

33. The womb? Childhood?

and all kinds of herds and flocks.

Further, much accrued to me as a result of the love of me. He appointed me ruler of a tribe, the best in his country. Provisions were assigned to me as daily fare: wine for the day's needs, boiled meat and roast fowl, over and above the game of the desert—for animals were snared for me and delivered to me, over and above the tribute of my hounds. Much date-wine was made for me, and milk was used in all cooking.

Thus I spent many years, and my sons became mighty men, each one controlling his tribe. The envoy who went north, or south to the Residence, stopped on my account;[34] I entertained everybody. I used to give water to the thirsty, and set on the road him who had lost his way, and I rescued and robbed. When the Bedouins regrettably ventured to oppose the kings of the foreign lands, I devised their [the kings'] course of action. The King of Retjenu made me spend many years as commander of his army. Every country that I marched against, I conquered, and it was driven away from the pasture of its wells; I took its cattle as spoil, I brought back its inhabitants and took away their food, and killed people in it, by my strength of arm, by my bow, by my movements and by my effectual plans. He valued me, and loved me, for he knew that I was brave. He placed me at the head of his children, for he saw that my hands prospered.

A mighty man of Retjenu came to challenge me in my tent. He was a champion unequaled; he had beaten the whole of Retjenu, and intended to fight with me. He expected to plunder me and planned to take my herds and flocks as spoil, by the advice of his tribe.

That King [Amem-nenshi] took counsel with me, and I said, "I do not know him, indeed I am not an associate of his, one who walks freely in his camp. Is it the case that I have opened his door, or overleaped his walls? It is jealousy, because he sees me executing your business. But I am like a bull of a free-pasturing herd in the midst of another herd, whom a steer of the herd charges and a long-

---

34. To receive and deliver messages, presumably.

horned bull attacks.[35] Is there a humble man who is loved when he becomes a superior? No barbarian becomes a friend of a man from the Egyptian Delta. What can fasten a papyrus plant to a rock? If a bull loves to fight, should a fierce bull turn his back in fear that he might be defeated? If he is minded to fight, let him say what he wants. Is God ignorant of what he has ordained? Does a man know how the matter stands?"

After my night's rest I strung my bow and tried my arrows; I made my dagger easy in its sheath, and polished my weapons. When it dawned all Retjenu came. It had stirred up its tribes, and assembled the peoples on its borders; it had planned this fight. Then he came to me, while I waited; I had placed myself near him. Every heart burned for me; the women and even the men jabbered. Everyone was sorry for me, and said, "Is there another mighty man who can fight against him?"[36] Then his shield, his axe and his armful of spears fell down before me, when I had escaped from his weapons and caused his arrows to pass by me, so that nothing remained. Each approached the other. He charged at me, and I shot him, my arrow sticking in his neck. He shrieked and fell on his nose. I dispatched him with his own axe, and sent forth my war-cry on his back, while every Asiatic shouted; and I gave praise to Montu,[37] while his partisans mourned for him. This King Amemnenshi took me to his bosom. Then I brought away his property; I took his herds and flocks as spoil. What he had planned to do to me, I did to him. I carried off what was in his tent, and stripped his camp. I became greater thereby: my wealth increased, my cattle became more numerous.

Thus has God done, to pardon him with whom he had been vexed when he strayed to another country! Today he is appeased.

A fugitive flees because of his affairs;
But my good repute is in the Residence.

---

35. Sinuhe speaks of himself as an isolated alien in the land. The rest of his speech is very obscure. The translation reflects the interpretation of Miriam Lichtheim, *Ancient Egyptian Literature, Volume I: The Old and Middle Kingdoms* (Berkeley and Los Angeles: University of California Press, 1973), p. 227.
36. The challenger.
37. A warlike god.

A lingerer lingers because of hunger;
But I give bread to my neighbor.
A man leaves his land because of nakedness;
But I have white garments and fine linen.
A man runs about for lack of one whom he can send;
But I have many slaves.
My house is beautiful,
My seat is easy;
The memory of me is in the Palace.

O whatever god ordained this flight, do thou shew mercy and return me to the Residence! Perhaps thou wilt let me see the place in which my heart dwells! What is more important than that I should be buried in Egypt, since I was born there? This is an appeal for help. May good fortune befall, may God grant me peace, may he do thus to perfect the end of him whom he has afflicted, taking pity on him who he cast out to live Abroad! Is he now appeased? May he hear the prayer of one far away! May he turn away his hand from him whom he sent roaming the earth, back to the place whence he drew it forth![38] May the King of Egypt be gracious to me! One lives by his grace. May I salute the Lady of the Land[39] who is in his palace, may I hear the affairs of her children! So shall my body grow young again, for now old age has descended and infirmity has overtaken me; my eyes are heavy, my hands are weak, my feet have slackened, my heart inclines to weariness. I am near to passing away, when they shall conduct me to the City of Eternity.[40] May I serve the Mistress of All![39] Then may she tell me that it is well with her children. May she spend eternity over me![41]

Now His Majesty, the King of southern and northern Egypt, Kheperkare,[42] had been told about these circumstances in which I was; and His Majesty kept sending to me with gifts of the royal

---

38. May the god who stretched out a punitive hand to Sinuhe return it to his bosom.
39. The Queen.
40. The cemetery.
41. A reference to the Queen as Sinuhe's "heaven"; see the King's letter which follows.
42. "Throne-name" of King Sesostris I (about 1970–1936 B.C.E.)

bounty, that he might rejoice this servant like the king of any foreign country. And the King's children, who were in his palace, let me hear of their affairs.

COPY OF THE LETTER[43] WHICH WAS BROUGHT TO THIS SERVANT TO BRING HIM BACK TO EGYPT

Horus, Life of Birth; Two-Ladies, Life of Birth; King of southern and northern Egypt, Kheperkare; son of Re, Sesostris,[44] may he live for ever and ever!

A royal letter to the attendant Sinuhe.

See, this letter of the King is brought to you to remind you that you have wandered about in foreign countries. You went forth from Kedmi to Retjenu. It was by your own heart's device that one land passed you on to another. What had you done that you should be opposed? You had not uttered sedition, that your speech should be reproved. You had not condemned the policy of the Councillors, that your utterances should be gainsaid. This idea carried your heart away; it was not in my heart against you."

This your Heaven,[45] who is in the Palace, continues and flourishes still. Her head is covered with the royalty of the land. Her children are in the Royal Apartments; you shall heap up good things of their gift, you shall live by their bounty.

Return to Egypt, that you may see the Residence, in which you grew up. You shall kiss the ground at the great Double Door, you shall join the Companions.

For now you have begun to grow infirm, you have lost your virile strength. Think of the day of embalmment, of passing to beatitude, when a night shall be appointed for you with cedar oil, and wrappings from the hands of Tayet;[46] how a funeral cortège shall be made for you on the day of burial, with a gilded mummy-case and a

---

43. Actually "decree"; kings' letters are always so called.
44. These are the titles and names of King Sesostris.
45. The Queen.
46. The oil and wrappings are for mummification; Tayet is the goddess of textile work.

head-piece[47] [inlaid] with blue, a canopy over you, and you placed in a hearse, oxen drawing you and singers going before you. Funeral dances shall be performed at the door of your tomb, and the list of offerings shall be recited for you; beasts shall be slaughtered at the doors of your tombstones, the pillars of your tomb being built of limestone, among the tombs of the King's children. You must not die abroad. Asiatics shall not conduct you [to your burial-place]; you shall not be placed in a sheep-skin and a tumulus made for you.[48] This is over-long to roam abroad. Consider [mortal] sickness, and come back.

This letter reached me while I was standing in the midst of my tribe. It was read to me, and I threw myself on my belly and touched the earth [with my forehead], and strewed it on my hair. I went round my camp rejoicing, saying, "How should this be done for a subject whom his heart has led astray to barbarous lands? The clemency is good indeed which has delivered me from death! Your good pleasure will allow me to meet my end, my body being in the Residence!"

COPY OF THE ANSWER TO THIS LETTER

The servant of the Palace, Sinuhe, says:

In very fair peace! This flight which this servant made unwittingly is known to your spirit, O good god, Lord of the Two Lands, whom Re loves and whom Montu, Lord of Thebes, favors. Amun, Lord of the Thrones of the Two Lands, Sobk-Re, Horus, Hathor, Atum and his Nine Gods, Sopdu-Neferbau, Semseru, Horus the Eastern, the Lady of Yemet—may she enfold your head!—the Conclave upon the waters, Min-Horus amid the foreign lands, Wereret, Lady of Pwenet, Nut, Harwer-Re, all the gods of Egypt and the Islands of the Sea,[49] may they give life and joy to your nostrils, may

---

47. A cover for the mummy's head and shoulders, having for the hair and eyebrows inlaid blue glaze simulating lapis lazuli.

48. Which is how he would be buried in Asia.

49. The Greek islands.

they endow you with their gifts, may they give you eternity without limit and everlasting without bounds; may the fear of you be noised abroad in lowlands and highlands—you have subdued all that the sun encircles! Such is the prayer of this servant for his Lord, who saves from the West.[50]

The lord of perception, who perceives the people, he perceived in the Court what this servant feared to say,[51] being like something to report which is grave. O great god, peer of Re in making one who works for himself wise, this servant is in the care of one who takes counsel concerning him; I am placed under his guidance. Your Majesty is Horus the Conqueror; your hands are victorious over all lands.

Let now Your Majesty command that I be allowed to bring Meki from southern Kedmi, Yaush out of Keshu, Menus from the lands of the Phœnicians;[52] they are kings of renowned names, who have grown up in the love of you. I will not mention Retjenu; it belongs to you like your very hounds.

This flight which your servant made, I did not foresee it, it was not in my mind, I did not plan it; I do not know what parted me from my place. It was like the condition of a dream, like a man of the Delta seeing himself in Elephantine, a man of the northern marshes in Nubia. I did not take fright, no one pursued me, I heard no reviling phrase, my name was not heard in the mouth of the reporter. But my flesh crept, while my feet scurried, my heart taking control of me, the god who ordained this flight urging me. I am not haughty. . . .[53]

Re has set the fear of you throughout the land [of Egypt], the dread of you in every foreign country. Whether I am at the Residence or whether I am here it is you who veil this horizon, and the sun rises at your pleasure. The water in the rivers, it is drunk when you wish; the air of heaven, it is breathed at your bidding.

This servant will hand over the Viziership which he has exer-

---

50. The place of death.
51. His yearning to return to Egypt.
52. Nothing more is known about these kings.
53. An obscure phrase is omitted.

cised here. Your Majesty will act as you please; one lives but by breath of your giving. Re, Horus and Hathor love those august nostrils[54] of yours which Montu, Lord of Thebes, desires shall live forever.

This servant was sent for; I was allowed to spend a day in Ya'a for handing over my property to my children, my eldest son being in charge of my tribe, all my property being in his possession—my serfs, all my herds and flocks, my fruit stores and every fruit-tree of mine. Then this servant came thence southwards. I halted at the Roads of Horus,[55] and the commandant there in charge of the frontier-patrol sent a message to the Residence to report. Then His Majesty sent a competent overseer of peasants of the Royal Domain, followed by laden ships bearing the King's bounty for the Bedouins who had come in charge of me, conducting me to the Roads of Horus. I presented each one by name. Every serving-man was at his task. I set forth and hoisted sail, and they kneaded and strained[56] beside me, until I reached the vicinity of Yet-towe.[57]

And the next morning, very early, they came to summon me, ten men coming and ten men going, to conduct me to the Palace. I touched the ground with my forehead between the sphinxes;[58] the King's children were standing in the doorway to meet me, and the Companions, who had been admitted to the forecourt of the Palace, set me on the way to the Royal Apartments. I found His Majesty upon a gilded throne. Then I stretched myself upon my belly, and was quite overcome before him. This god greeted me kindly, but I was like a man carried off in the dust: my soul fainted, my flesh quaked, my heart was not in my body that I should know life from death. Then His Majesty said to one of the Companions, "Raise him up, let him speak to me." And His Majesty said, "So you have returned after roaming foreign lands. Flight has conquered you;

---

54. The nose was for the Egyptians the organ of life.
55. On the frontier between Palestine and Egypt, close to the modern El-Kantarah.
56. Operations of beer-making, carried out in a boat beside that in which Sinuhe was traveling.
57. The Residence at the time, about forty miles south of Cairo.
58. At the great Double Door.

you have grown infirm, you have reached old age. It is no small matter that your body should be buried without your being escorted to your grave by barbarians. Don't act against your own interests, silent one! You did not speak when your name was mentioned."

I feared punishment, and I made answer with the answer of one afraid: "What does my Lord say to me? [If I knew,] then I would answer it. There is nothing I can do. Dread is the hand of God; it is in my body like that which brought about the predestined flight. See, I am before you, life is yours. May Your Majesty do as you wish."

Then the King's children were allowed to be brought in; and His Majesty said to the Queen, "See, Sinuhe has returned as an Asiatic whom Bedouins have formed." She uttered a very loud cry, while the King's children all shouted at once; and they said to His Majesty, "It is not really he, O Sovereign, my Lord?" And His Majesty said, "It is really he."

Now they had brought their necklaces and their sistra and their rattles[59] with them, and they held them out to His Majesty:

Let your hands rest on what is beautiful, O enduring King,
On the adornments of the Lady of Heaven,

That the Golden One may give life to your nostrils,
That the Lady of the Stars[60] may enfold you.

May the Crown of southern Egypt fare northwards,
The Crown of northern Egypt fare southwards,
And be united and joined by Your Majesty's utterance.

Ujoyet[61] is set upon your brow.
You have removed your subjects from evil.

---

59. These are all emblems of Hathor, the goddess of love, beauty and joy.
60. Three epithets of Hathor.
61. The cobra or *uraeus* goddess of northern Egypt.

May Re show you grace, O Lord of the Two Lands;
Hail to you, as to the Lady of All.[62]

Unstring your bow, put up your arrow,
Give breath to him who is stifling.

Give us our good festal expenses in this sheikh,[63] a son of
    Mehyet,[64]
A barbarian born in Egypt!

He took to flight through fear of you,
He left the land through dread of you.

May the face of him who has seen your face not be turned
    away;
May the eye that has looked at you not be afraid.

And His Majesty said, "He shall not fear, he shall not fall into
dread. He shall be a Companion among the Councillors, he shall be
placed in the midst of the Courtiers. Go along to the apartments of
purification, to wait upon him."

Then I went forth from the interior of the Royal Apartments, the
King's children giving me their hands. Afterwards we went to the
great Double Door. And I was placed in the house of a king's son,
in which were fine things, and in which was a bath-room, and
images of the Horizon,[65] and valuables from the Treasury, and garments of royal linen; and myrrh and fine oil of the King, and of the
Councillors whom he loves, were in every room. Every serving-
man was at his task.

The years were made to pass away from my body; I was shaved,
and my hair was combed. A burden was given back to the desert—

---

62. The Queen.
63. The children playfully ask for Sinuhe to be pardoned and given to them instead
of something with which to celebrate the joyous day of his return.
64. A dolphin goddess of the north of Egypt.
65. Obscure.

my clothes to the Sandfarers. I was clothed in fine linen, and anointed with fine oil; I lay down at night upon a bed. I gave the sand to those who dwell on it, and wood-oil to him who would anoint himself with it.

There was given to me the house of the lord of an estate, one that had been in the possession of a Companion. Many artisans restored it, all its woodwork being put into repair anew. Meals were brought to me from the Palace, three and four times a day, over and above what the King's children gave, without a moment of cessation.

A pyramid was built for me[66] of stone, in the midst of the pyramids. The stonemasons who fashion pyramids divided up its ground plan among them. The master-draftsmen drew in it, the master-sculptors carved in it, the master-builders who are on the desert occupied themselves with it. It was supplied with all the equipment which is placed in a tomb-chamber. I was given *ka*-servants,[67] and a desert-garden was made for me, in which was land better than that of the town, like what is made for a Chief Companion. My statue[68] was covered with gold, its kilt with electrum.

It is His Majesty who caused this to be done. There is no poor man for whom the like has been done. And I am enjoying the favors of the King's bounty until the arrival of the day of "landing."[69]

It has been copied from beginning to end, according to what was found in writing.

---

66. The King was better than his word; previously only an ordinary "tomb" had been mentioned. Pyramids were usually reserved for the royal family.

67. Persons who maintain the cult of the dead with food offerings, recital of spells, and so on.

68. Placed in the tomb.

69. Dying, from a traveler by water reaching his journey's end.

Tales of the Magicians

These are known from only one manuscript, a much damaged papyrus, without beginning or end, at Berlin. Its date is about 1600 B.C.E., in the "Hyksos Period," but the stories it contains may be much earlier.

It is not hard to reconstruct the beginning. King Cheops, the second king of the powerful Fourth Dynasty and builder of the Great Pyramid, who reigned 2589–2566 B.C.E., is one day in need of entertainment. Calling his sons before him, he desires them to amuse him with stories of magical feats performed in the reigns of former kings. In the part that is left each son in turn stands up and tells his tale, after which Cheops commands that offerings be made to the soul of the king in whose reign the marvel occurred, and also an offering (relatively insignificant) to the soul of the magician who performed the marvel. How many tales are lost at the beginning it is impossible to say; but the number of Cheops' sons was not great, and it may well be that a tale of which we have only the last lines (immediately preceding the story of Weba-aner), in which Cheops has offerings made to King Djoser and his "chief ritualist" (probably Imhotep), was the first. Afer two other narratives connected with predecessors of Cheops a contemporary magician is produced, who also works wonders. Thereafter the narrative takes on a quite different character, having nothing to do with magicians and their feats; this part is therefore not translated.

The magicians Weba-aner and Djedjaemankh bear a title which I have translated "chief ritualist," and which means literally "chief holder of the ritual book." The bearers of this title were a class of priests who, being in the habit of reciting spells of all sorts from the books in question, were specialists in magic. The title, after becoming synonymous with "magician," "diviner," persisted in abbreviated form until very late times, and was taken into Hebrew, occurring often in Genesis and Exodus with reference to Egyptian practitioners.

Owing to gaps in the manuscript it has been necessary to reconstruct the narrative in some places.

I

... THEN THE KING'S son Khafre[1] stood up to speak, and said, "I will let Your Majesty hear a marvel which took place in the reign of your forefather the late King Nebka,[2] when he went to the temple of Ptah, Lord of Anekhtowe.[3]

"And His Majesty went to confer with the chief ritualist Weba-aner. Now Weba-aner's wife had fallen in love with a certain towns-man. And she sent him a boxful of beautiful clothes... then he came back with the maidservant.

"Now when some days had passed by this—now there was a garden-house by Weba-aner's lake—then the townsman said to Weba-aner's wife, 'Why, there is a garden-house by Weba-aner's lake; see, let us spend a time in it.' And Weba-aner's wife sent a message to the steward who was in charge of the lake, saying, 'Let the garden-house which is by the lake be made ready.' And she spent the day there, drinking and eating with the townsman until the sun went down. Now when evening had come he went down to the lake [to bathe]. And the maidservant went to the steward and reported to him what had happened with Weba-aner's wife.

"Now when it had dawned and a second day had come, the stew-

---

1. Greek Chephren, the next king but one after Cheops and builder of the Second Pyramid at Gizah.
2. A king of the Third Dynasty, his date uncertain.
3. A district or suburb of Memphis.

ard went to the chief ritualist Weba-aner and recounted the whole of this matter to him. . . .

"Then Weba-aner said, 'Bring me my box of ebony inlaid with electrum. . . .' And he modeled a crocodile of wax, seven handbreadths long. And he recited a magic spell over it, and said to it, 'Now when he comes to bathe in my lake according to his daily habit, you must seize the townsman for me.' Then he gave it to the steward, and said to him, 'Now when the townsman goes down to the lake according to his daily habit, then you must throw this crocodile into the water after him.' The steward went off, taking the wax crocodile with him.

"Then Weba-aner's wife sent to the steward in charge of the lake, saying, 'Let the garden-house which is by the lake be made ready, for I am coming to sit in it.' And the garden-house was made ready with all good things. Then they[4] went off, and made holiday with the townsman.

"Now when evening had come the townsman came to the lake according to his daily habit. Then the steward threw the wax crocodile after him into the water; and it became a crocodile seven cubits[5] long, and it seized the townsman, and carried him off.

"Now Weba-aner was detained with His Majesty, King Nebka, for seven days, the townsman being kept in the deepest place of the lake, without breathing. And when the seven days had passed, King Nebka proceeded to the temple. Then the chief ritualist Weba-aner placed himself in the royal presence, and said to His Majesty . . . . 'May Your Majesty go and see this marvel that has happened in Your Majesty's reign to a townsman.' And His Majesty went with Weba-aner. Then Weba-aner conjured the crocodile, saying, 'Bring the townsman here.' And the crocodile came forth, bringing the townsman, to the place where they were. . . . And His Majesty King Nebka said, 'No doubt this crocodile is dangerous.' Then Weba-aner stooped down and took it up, and it was a wax crocodile in his hand.

"And the chief ritualist Weba-aner reported to His Majesty King

---

4. Apparently Weba-aner's wife and her maidservant.
5. 12 feet 2 inches.

Nebka this thing that the townsman had done with his wife on his premises. Then His Majesty said to the crocodile, 'Take to yourself what is your own,' and the crocodile went down to the depth of the lake, and no one knew where he went with him.

"Then His Majesty King Nebka had Weba-aner's wife brought to a piece of land north of the Residence, and burnt her, and her ashes were thrown into the river.

"That is a marvel which took place in the reign of your forefather, King Nebka, a feat of the chief ritualist Weba-aner."

And His Majesty King Cheops said, "Let a thousand loaves of bread, and a hundred jugs of beer, and one ox, and two bags of incense, be offered to the late King Nebka; and also let one cake, and one jug of beer, and a large piece of meat, and one bag of incense, be given to the chief ritualist Weba-aner, for I have seen an example of his [magical] knowledge."

And it was done exactly as His Majesty commanded.

II

Then the King's son Baufre[6] stood up to speak, and said, "I will let Your Majesty hear a marvel which took place in the reign of your father, the late Snefru,[7] a feat of the chief ritualist Djedjaemankh, a story of yesterday, of recent times. . . .

"It happened that His Majesty was worried, and he set the courtiers of the Royal Household to seek out a means of refreshment for him, and he did not find it. And he said, 'Go, bring me the chief ritualist, the book-scribe, Djedjaemankh.' And he was brought to him at once. And His Majesty told him, 'I have set the courtiers of the Royal Household to seek out a means of refreshment for me, and I have not found it.'

"And Djedjaemankh said to him, 'Let Your Majesty go to the lake of the Great House, when a boat has been "manned" for you with all the fairest women of the interior of your palace. And Your Majesty's

---

6. Not known from any other source.
7. The immediate predecessor of Cheops and founder of the Fourth Dynasty. Date about 2720 B.C.E.

heart will be refreshed by seeing them row up and down, while you look at the beautiful thickets of your lake, and look at its beautiful marshes and banks; your heart will be refreshed by it.'

"Then His Majesty said, 'But I will arrange my boating trip. Let me be brought twenty ebony oars, inlaid with gold, their handles being of *sekeb*-[8]wood overworked with electrum. And let me be brought twenty women, beautiful in body, with shapely breasts and braided tresses, who have not yet had children, and also let twenty nets be brought to me, and let these nets be given to these women to wear, when their clothes have been taken off.' And it was done exactly as His Majesty commanded.

"And they rowed up and down, and His Majesty was happy at seeing them row. Then one of them, who was at the stern,[9] entangled her tresses, and a hair-ornament of new[10] turquoise fell into the water. Then she stopped rowing; and her side stopped rowing. And His Majesty said to them, 'Aren't you rowing?' And they said, 'Our "stroke" has stopped rowing.' And His Majesty said to her, 'Why aren't you rowing?' And she said, 'Because a hair-ornament of new turquoise has fallen into the water.' Then His Majesty said to her, 'See, I will give you one like it.' And she said, 'I prefer my own property to a copy of it.'

"And His Majesty said, 'Go, bring me the chief ritualist Djedjaemankh.' And he was brought to him at once. And His Majesty said, 'Djedjaemankh, my brother,[11] I did as you said, and My Majesty's heart was refreshed at seeing them row. Then a hair-ornament of new turquoise, belonging to one of the "strokes," fell into the water. And she stopped rowing, with the result that she upset her side. And I said to her, "Why aren't you rowing?" She said to me, "Because a hair-ornament of new turquoise has fallen into the water." I said to her, "Row on; see, I will replace it." And she said to me, "I prefer my own property to a copy of it."'

---

8. An unknown kind.

9. And was therefore "stroke," giving the time to the other rowers on her side of the boat.

10. Turquoise is at its best when newly mined; it tends to fade after a certain time.

11. Snefru was later celebrated for the geniality and simplicity of his manners, as well as his beneficence.

"Then the chief ritualist Djedjaemankh uttered a magical spell; and he placed one side of the waters of the lake upon the other side of them; and he found the hair-ornament lying on a potsherd. Then he brought it, and gave it to its mistress. Now the water, it had been twelve cubits deep along its middle, but it ended up at 24 cubits after being doubled back. Then he uttered a magical spell, and brought the waters of the lake back to their former position. And His Majesty spent the day making holiday with the whole of the royal household. And he then rewarded the chief ritualist Djedjaemankh with all good things.

"That is a marvel which took place in the reign of your father, the late King Snefru, a feat of the chief ritualist, the book-scribe Djedjaemankh."

And His Majesty King Cheops said, "Let a thousand loaves of bread, and a hundred jugs of beer, and one ox, and two bags of incense, be offered to His Majesty the late King Snefru; and also let one cake, and one jug of beer, and a large piece of meat, and one bag of incense be given to the chief ritualist, the book-scribe Djedjaemankh, for I have seen an example of his [magical] knowledge."

And it was done exactly as His Majesty commanded.

III

Then the King's son Hordedef[12] stood up to speak, and said, "Hitherto Your Majesty has heard examples of [magical] knowledge only as something which those who have passed away could do, and it is not known if they are true—not deeds of a man under Your Majesty, in your own time, who is unknown to you."

And His Majesty said, "What are they, Hordedef, my son?"

Then the King's son, Hordedef, said, "There is a townsman, Djedi by name, who dwells in the town of Ded-snefru.[13] He is a townsman 110 years old, who still eats 500 loaves, a shoulder of

---

12. Famous as a sage and author of books of wisdom. His tomb (at Gizah) is known.
13. Position unknown except that it was south of the place (presumably Memphis) where these tales were told to the king.

beef, and drinks 100 jugs of beer [daily]. He knows how to fasten on a head that has been cut off, and he knows how to make a lion walk behind him, with its leash on the ground. And he knows the number of the secret chambers of the sanctuary of Thoth."[14]

Now His Majesty King Cheops was always searching for the secret chambers of the sanctuary of Thoth, to make a copy of them for his "horizon."[15] And His Majesty said, "You yourself, Hordedef, my son, shall bring him to me."

Then ships were made ready for the King's son Hordedef, and he went southwards to Ded-snefru. Now when the ships had been moored at the quay, he journeyed by land, reposing in a litter of ebony, the carrying-poles being of another wood, and further overlaid with gold. Now when he reached Djedi the litter was set down, and Hordedef stood up to greet him. He found him lying on a mat at his threshold, one slave at his head, massaging him, another rubbing his feet.

Then the King's son Hordedef said,[16] "May your condition be like that of one who lives before growing infirm—although old age is the occasion of "landing," the occasion of being embalmed, the occasion of being buried—one who sleeps until daylight, free from sickness. . . . This is the greeting to the revered one. I have come here to summon you, on business of my father Cheops. You shall eat the dainties of the King's giving, the choice fare of his followers; and he will conduct you after a happy life to your fathers who are in the cemetery."

And this Djedi said, "In peace, in peace, Hordedef, King's son whom your father loves! May your father Cheops favor you! May he advance your place to be among the elders. May your soul contend successfully with your enemy! May your spirit learn the ways which lead to the gate of Hebesbag![17] This is the salutation to the King's son!"

Then the King's son Hordedef stretched out his hands to him,

---

14. The god of wisdom and learning.
15. That is, his pyramid, which bore the name "Cheops is one belonging to the horizon."
16. These greetings are very high-falutin and difficult to translate.
17. A guardian of the entrance to the Underworld.

and raised him up; and he proceeded with him to the quay, giving him his hand. And Djedi said, "Let me be given a boat which may bring me my children with my books." Then two boats with their crews were put at his disposal. But Djedi came northwards in the traveling-boat in which the King's son Hordedef was.

Now when he reached the Residence the King's son Hordedef went in to report to His Majesty King Cheops; and he said, "My Lord Sovereign—may you live, prosper, and be healthy—I have brought Djedi." And His Majesty proceeded to the pillared hall of the Great House; and Djedi was ushered in to him.

And His Majesty said, "How is it, Djedi, that I have not seen you?"

And Djedi said, "It is he who is summoned who comes, my Lord Sovereign—May you live, prosper, and be healthy! Having been summoned, see, I have come."

And His Majesty said, "Is what is said true, that you can fasten on a head that has been cut off?"

And Djedi said, "Yes, I can, my Lord Sovereign."

And His Majesty said, "Let me be brought a prisoner who is in the prison when his doom has been inflicted."

And Djedi said, "But not to men, my lord Sovereign! See, it is forbidden to do such a thing to the 'Noble Herd.'"[18]

Then a goose was brought to him with its head cut off. And the goose was placed on the western side of the pillared hall, its head on the eastern side of the hall. Then Djedi uttered a magical spell, and the goose rose up quivering, and its head too. And when one had reached the other, the goose stood up cackling. Then he had another kind of goose brought to him, and the same was done with it. Then His Majesty had an ox brought to him, its head having been struck off to the ground. And Djedi uttered a magical spell, and then the bull stood up lowing.

After this it was told how a lion was brought in, and Djedi made it "follow him, its leash fallen to the ground"; *but only these last words are in the manuscript, the preceding ones having been omitted by negligence.*

---

18. The human race, "God's flock," as an early king calls it.

The Tale of the Two Brothers

This story is contained in only one manuscript, which is now preserved in the British Museum and named the Papyrus D'Orbiney after its former owner. The papyrus dates from the end of the Nineteenth Dynasty (ca. 1200 B.C.E.) and contains nineteen pages of beautiful cursive writing. The story is a complex literary creation based loosely on an Upper Egyptian myth concerning the gods Anubis, god of mummification and guardian of the necropolis, and Bata, a little-known god primarily associated with pastoralism. The story has provided a rich source for folklorists, who have discovered a number of themes in it that are also found in other ancient literatures. The most important of these is the so-called "Potiphar's Wife" theme—a would-be adulteress who defends herself by falsely accusing the man who refused her—that is found both in the story of Joseph in the book of Genesis and in the fifth century B.C.E. Athenian dramatist Euripides' tragedy *Hippolytus*.

Now there were once, they say, two brothers, of the same father and mother; Anupu was the name of the elder, and Bata the name of the younger. Now Anupu had a house and a wife, and his younger brother lived with him like a son. It was he who made clothes for him, and drove his cattle to the fields. And it was he who did the plowing and harvested for him, and he who did all the work that there is in fields. Now the younger brother was a comely lad; there was not his like in all the land; and the might of a god was in him.

And Anupu's younger brother tended his cattle according to his daily wont, and went home to his house each evening laden with all manner of herbs of the field, and with milk and wood, and all good things of the field, and set them down before his elder brother, who was sitting with his wife, and drank and ate, and went out to sleep in his cow-house among his cattle, alone.

Now when it had dawned and another day was come, the younger brother brought food which had been cooked and set it down before his elder brother, who gave him provisions for the fields; and he collected his cattle to pasture them in the fields, and he drove them out, and they said to him, "The grass of such-and-such a place is good," and he understood all that they said and took them off to the good place with the grass that they desired. And the cattle that he tended became very fine, and they increased their calving very much.

Now at the time of the plowing his elder brother said to him, "Make ready for us a good span of oxen for plowing, for the land has come forth[1] and it is good for plowing. Also come to the field with seed, for we shall be busy plowing tomorrow"—so he said to him. And his younger brother did just as his elder brother had told him to do.

Now when it had dawned and another day was come, they went to the field with their seed, and busied themselves with plowing, and they were very happy in their work at the beginning of their labors.

Now some time after this they were in the field, and they were held up for seed, and Anupu sent his younger brother, saying, "Go and fetch us seed from the village." And Bata found his elder brother's wife sitting doing her hair; and he said to her, "Get up and give

1. Has emerged after the annual inundation.

me some seed, that I may go back to the field, because my elder brother will be waiting for me; don't make me wait." And she said to him, "Go and open the granary and bring away what you want; don't make me interrupt my hair-dressing."

And the lad went into his cow-house, and brought a large vessel, wishing to take away much seed; and he loaded himself up with barley and spelt and came out with them.

And she said to him, "What is the amount that's on your shoulder?" And he told her, "It's three bushels of spelt and two bushels of barley, five bushels in all, that are on my shoulder"—so he told her. And she talked with him, saying, "There is great strength in you; for I see your feats daily." And she desired to know him as a male is known, and she stood up and took hold of him, and said to him, "Come, let us spend an hour lying down. It will be well for you—then I will make you fine clothes."

And the lad became like a panther of southern Egypt for great anger at the evil speech that she had uttered to him. And she was very much afraid. And he talked with her, saying, "But see, you are like a mother to me, and your husband is like a father to me, and he, who is older than I, it is he who has brought me up. What is this great crime that you have mentioned to me? Do not say it to me again, and I will tell it to no one. I will not let it come out of my mouth to anyone." And he lifted up his burden and went off to the field. And he reached his elder brother, and they busied themselves in their labors.

Now afterwards, at evening-time, his elder brother went home to his house, while Bata tended his cattle and loaded himself with all manner of things of the field, and brought his cattle back before him to put them into their cow-house in the village for the night.

Now his elder brother's wife was afraid because of the speech that she had uttered; and she brought fat and grease,[2] and feigned to have been beaten, with the intent to say to her husband, "It is your younger brother who has beaten me."

And her husband came back in the evening, according to his

---

2. Why? For use as a salve? As an emetic (see below)?

daily wont, and he reached his house, and found his wife lying
down pretending to be in pain; she did not pour water over his
hands according to his wont, nor had she lighted the lamp before
he came in, and his house was in darkness, and she was lying vom-
iting. And her husband said to her, "Who has been speaking with
you?" Then she said to him, "No one has been speaking with me
except your younger brother. When he came to fetch away seed for
you and found me sitting alone he said to me, "Come, let us spend
an hour lying down. Put on your wig," he said to me, and I did not
listen to him. "Am I not your mother, and is not your brother like a
father to you?" I said to him. And he was afraid, and he beat me to
prevent me from reporting it to you. Now if you let him live I will
kill myself. See, when he comes back, do not speak to him, because
if I were to make this ugly accusation [before him] he would turn it
into an injury."

And his elder brother became like a panther of southern Egypt
[for anger], and he sharpened his spear, and took it in his hand, and
he stood behind the door of his cow-house to kill his younger brother when he should return in the evening to drive his cattle into the
cow-house.

Now when the sun set Bata loaded himself with all manner of
herbs of the field, according to his daily wont, and came back; and
the foremost cow entered the cow-house, and said to her herdsman, "See, your elder brother is standing in front of you with his
spear to kill you. Flee before him." And he understood what his
foremost cow had said; and the next one went in and said the same
thing. And he looked under the door of his cow-house, and saw the
feet of his elder brother as he stood behind the door with his spear
in his hand. And he set his burden down on the ground and betook
himself to speedy flight. And his elder brother went after him with
his spear.

And his younger brother prayed to Re-Harakhte,[3] saying, "My
good lord, thou art he who judges between the evildoer and the just

---

3. A composite solar deity, combining Re "the Sun" and Harákhte "the Horus of the
Horizon."

man." Then Re heard all his appeal, and created a great water between him and his elder brother, full of crocodiles, and one of them found himself on one side, the other on the other. And the elder brother struck twice on his hands[4] because of not having killed him. And the younger brother called to him from the other side, saying, "Stay here until dawn, and when the sun rises you and I will be judged before him, and he will deliver the evildoer to the righteous; for I will never live with you again, nor be in any place where you are. I will go to the Valley of the Cedar."[5]

Now when it had dawned and another day was come, Re-Harakhte arose, and they saw one another. And the lad spoke with his elder brother, saying, "Why did you pursue me to kill me wrongfully, before you had heard what I had to say? For I am indeed your younger brother, and you are like a father to me, and your wife is like a mother to me; is it not so? Now when you sent me to fetch seed for us, your wife said to me, 'Come, let us spend an hour lying down'; but see, to you she has turned it into the opposite."

And he informed him of everything that had happened between him and his wife; and he swore by Re-Harakhte, saying, "Your coming with your spear to kill me wrongfully was at the bidding of a whore." And he took a reed-knife, and cut off his privy member, and threw it into the water, and a shad-fish swallowed it. And he grew faint and became weak. And his elder brother was very sorry for him, and stood weeping aloud for him; he was not able to cross the water to where his younger brother was, because of the crocodiles.

And his younger brother called to him, saying, "Though you remember one bad matter, do you not remember one good one, or one thing that I have done for you? Go home, and collect your cattle, for I will not stay in any place where you are. I will go to the Valley of the Cedar. Now what you shall do for me is to come to help me, if you know that anything is wrong with me, for I shall take out

---

4. Expressing disappointment or frustration.
5. Now known to be a real place, in the Lebanon.

my heart, and place it on the top of the flower of the cedar. And if the cedar is cut down, and it [my heart] falls to the ground and you come to seek it, even if you spend seven years in seeking it do not be discouraged. And if you find it, and put it into a jar of cold water, then I shall come to life, and will take vengeance for being sinned against. And you will know if anything is wrong with me, when a mug of beer is given into your hand and it foams up. Then do not delay. Certainly it will happen to you."

And he went off to the Valley of the Cedar; and his elder brother went off to his house with his hand laid on his head, which was smeared with dust.[6] Then he arrived at his house, and he killed his wife, and threw her to the dogs. And he dwelt in mourning for his younger brother.

Now some time after this Bata was in the Valley of the Cedar, no one being with him; and he spent his days hunting the beasts of the desert, and in the evening he came back to lie down under the cedar, on the top of whose flower his heart was.

Now some time after this he built himself a castle with his own hands in the Valley of the Cedar, full of all good things, in order to set up a home for himself. Then he came out of his castle, and he encountered the Nine Gods,[7] walking and ordering the affairs of the whole world. And the Nine told one of themselves to say to him, "Hail Bata, Bull of the Nine, are you here alone, having left your town, fleeing from the wife of Anupu, your elder brother? See, he has killed his wife, and you are avenged on him for all the injuries done you." And they were very sorry for him. And Re-Harakhte said to Khnum, "Do you fashion a spouse for Bata, that he may not dwell alone."

And Khnum made him a spouse, who was more beautiful in body than any woman in all the world; the essence of every god was in

---

6. Tokens of mourning.

7. A group of four generations of gods, originating in Heliopolis and consisting of a solar god (here Re-Harákhte) at the head, with Show and Tefenet, Geb and Nut, Osiris, Isis, Seth and Nephthys. The number and constitution of the so-called "ennead" are, however, variable, so that we need not be surprised to find among them Khnum, who fashions mankind as a potter fashions jars upon a wheel.

her. And the Seven Hathors[8] came to see her; and they said with one voice, "She will have a sharp death."

And he loved her very much; and she dwelt in his house, and he spent his days hunting the beasts of the desert, bringing them and laying them before her. And he said to her, "Do not go outside lest the sea carry you off; for I shall not be able to save you from it, because I am a woman like you. Now my heart lies on the top of the flower of the cedar, and if anyone else finds it I shall fight with him." And he described his heart to her in all its detail.

Now some time after this Bata went to hunt, after his daily wont. Then the girl went out to walk about under the cedar, which was beside her house. Then the sea saw her, its waves beating after her, and she betook herself to flight before it and went into her house. And the sea called to the cedar, saying, "Seize her for me." And the cedar brought a lock of her hair. And the sea brought it to Egypt, and laid it at the place of the launderers of Pharaoh. And the smell of the lock of hair got into Pharaoh's clothes; and Pharaoh's servants quarreled with Pharaoh's launderers, saying, "Pharaoh's clothes smell of unguent." And they fell to quarreling with them every day, and they did not know what to do.

And Pharaoh's head launderer walked to the riverbank, and he was very wretched owing to the contention with him every day. And he stopped still and stood on the desert opposite the lock of hair, which was in the water; and he made a man go down, and he brought it to him. And he found its odor very sweet, and he took it to Pharaoh. And they fetched the scribes and learned men of Pharaoh; and they said to Pharaoh, "This lock of hair belongs to a daughter of Re-Harakhte in whom is the essence of every god. Now it is a present to you from another country. Send messengers to every foreign land to seek her; but the messenger who goes to the Valley of the Cedar, send many people with him to bring her back."[9]

Then His Majesty said, "What you have said is very good"; and

---

8. They were fabled to come to newborn children of importance, and predict the manner of their death.

9. It seems that, although the woman might be in any foreign country, it was thought most likely that she would be found in the Valley of the Cedar.

people were sent forth.

Now some time after this the people who had gone abroad came back to make report to His Majesty; but those who had gone to the Valley of the Cedar did not return, for Bata had killed them—but he spared one of them to make report to His Majesty. And His Majesty sent many foot-soldiers, and also chariotry, to fetch her back. And there was a woman among them into whose hand had been given all beautiful adornments of women. And the woman came back to Egypt with her, and there was rejoicing over her in all the land. And His Majesty loved her very much, and he gave her the rank of Great Favorite.

And he spoke with her to get her to describe her husband; and she said to His Majesty, "Have the cedar cut down and broken up." And he sent foot-soldiers with their weapons to cut down the cedar, and they reached the cedar and cut down the flower on which was Bata's heart, and he fell down dead at that very moment.

Now when it had dawned and another day was come, the cedar having been cut down, Anupu, the elder brother of Bata, went into his house and sat down to wash his hands. And a mug of beer was given to him, and it foamed up; and another, of wine, was given to him, and it turned sour. And he took up his staff and his sandals, also his clothes and his weapons, and set forth to journey to the Valley of the Cedar.

And he entered the castle of his younger brother, and found him lying on his couch, dead. And he wept when he saw his younger brother lying in death, and went to search for his heart under the cedar under which his younger brother went to sleep in the evening. And he spent three years in seeking it, without finding it. And when he had entered upon the fourth year, he longed to return to Egypt, and said, "I will go away tomorrow"—so he said in his heart.

Now when it had dawned and another day was come, he fell to walking under the cedar, and spent the day seeking the heart. And he went back in the evening, and spent a short time in seeking it again. And he found a berry, and went back with it. Now it was his younger brother's heart. And he fetched a jar of cold water and threw it into it, and he sat down according to his daily wont.

Now when night had come Bata's heart absorbed the water, and Bata quivered all over, and suddenly looked at his elder brother, while his heart was in the jar. And Anupu, his elder brother, took up the jar of cold water in which was his younger brother's heart, and it [the heart] had drunk it, and his heart stood in its place, and he became as he had been. And they embraced one another, and each of them spoke with his fellow. And Bata said to his elder brother, "See, I will become a great bull, with all beautiful markings, one the nature of which will not be known; and you shall sit on my back until the sun rises, and we are in the place where my wife is, that I may take vengeance. And you shall take me to the place where the King is, for all good things will be done for you, and you will be rewarded with silver and gold for having taken me to Pharaoh, for I shall become a great wonder, and they will rejoice over me in all the land, and you will go away to your village."

Now when it had dawned and another day was come, then Bata took on the form which he had told his brother about, and Anupu, his elder brother, sat on his back until dawn, and he reached the place where the King was. And His Majesty was informed about him, and he saw him, and he was very glad about him. And he made a great feast because of him, saying, "This is a great marvel that has happened"; and they rejoiced over him in all the land. And the King loaded him with silver and gold for his elder brother, who dwelt in his village; and the King gave him many people and much property, and Pharaoh loved him very much, more than anybody else in all the land.

Now some time after this the bull went into the dining-room, and stood where the Favorite was; and he fell to talking with her, saying, "See, I am still alive." And she said to him, "Who, pray, are you?" And he said to her, "I am Bata. I know that when you had the cedar broken up for Pharaoh it was on my account, so that I should not live; but see, I am still alive, being a bull." And the Favorite was very frightened at the announcement that her husband had made to her. And he went out of the dining-room.

And His Majesty sat making holiday with her, and she poured out wine for His Majesty; and the King was very happy with her. And she said to His Majesty, "Swear to me by God, saying, 'What the Favorite may say I will obey for her sake'"; and he hearkened to all that she said. "Let me be allowed to eat some of the liver of this bull, for he will be of no use," she said to him. And the King was very much vexed at what she had said, and Pharaoh was very sorry for him.

Now when it had dawned and another day was come, the King announced a great feast with sacrifice of the bull, and the King sent one of his chief butchers to have the bull dispatched. And afterwards he was dispatched; and while he was borne on the men's shoulders he shook his neck, and cast two drops of blood beside the two door-jambs of His Majesty—one of them fell on one side of the Great Portal of Pharaoh, and the other on the other side—and they grew into two large persea trees, and each of them was very fine. And they went to tell His Majesty, "Two large persea trees have grown up, a great marvel for His Majesty, in the night, beside His Majesty's Great Portal." And they rejoiced over them in all the land, and the King made offering to them.

Now some time after this His Majesty appeared at the Lapis-lazuli Window, with a garland of all manner of flowers at his neck; and he was in a gilded chariot, and he came out of the palace to see the persea trees. And the Favorite came out with horses, following Pharaoh. And His Majesty sat down under one of the persea trees, and the Favorite under the other. And Bata spoke with his wife, saying, "O you traitress, I am Bata, and I am alive in spite of you! I know of your having caused the cedar to be cut down for Pharaoh on my account, and I became a bull and you had me killed."

Now some time after this the Favorite stood pouring out wine for His Majesty, and the King was happy with her. And she said to His Majesty, "Swear to me by God, saying, 'What the Favorite may tell me I will obey for her sake,' so you shall say." And he hearkened to all that she said. And she said, "Have these two persea trees cut down, and made into beautiful furniture." And the King obeyed all that she said, and after a short time His Majesty sent cunning carpenters, and Pharaoh's persea trees were cut down. And the King's wife, the Favorite, watched. And a splinter flew up and entered the Favorite's mouth, and she swallowed it, and she conceived and became pregnant in the space of a moment. And the King did everything that she fancied with them [the trees].

Now some time after this she gave birth to a man-child, and they went to tell His Majesty, "A man-child has been born to you"; and he was fetched, and a nurse and female attendants were given him, and people rejoiced over him in all the land. And the King sat making holiday, and the people were jubilant. And His Majesty loved him at once, very much, and appointed him Viceroy of Nubia.

Now some time after this His Majesty made him Crown Prince of the whole land. Now some time after this, when he had spent many years as Crown Prince of the whole land, His Majesty flew up to heaven.[10]

And the [new] King said, "Let my great royal officials be brought to me, that I may inform them of everything that has happened to me." And his wife was brought to him, and he and she were judged before them, and they agreed with him.[11] And his elder brother was brought to him, and he made him Crown Prince of the whole land. And he spent thirty years as King of Egypt, and then passed away to Life.[12] And his elder brother arose in his place on the day of "landing."

It has come to an end happily and in peace. For the pleasure of the Scribe of Pharaoh's Treasury, Kagabu, the Scribe Hori and the Scribe Meremope. Made by the Scribe Innana, the owner of this book. As for him who speaks against this book, may Thoth be his adversary!

---

10. Died.
11. And so condemned her—to death, no doubt.
12. Died.

Rhampsinitus and the Clever Thief

About the middle of the fifth century B.C.E., Herodotus of Halicarnassus, the Greek "Father of History," visited Egypt briefly. The fruits of his visit are contained in the long account of Egypt and of Egyptian history in the second book of the *History of the Persian Wars*. As was common in Egypt in the first millennium B.C.E., the story of Rhampsinitus—Ramses, the son of Neith, the patron goddess of the city of Sais in the western Delta—is set in the time of one of the great kings of the past, probably the Nineteenth Dynasty king Ramses II (1279–1212 B.C.E.). The story of the clever thief who lives by his wits and wins the king's daughter is a folktale found in many cultures of the world. Herodotus' version, however, with its emphasis on the looting of royal wealth and the king's ability to recognize wisdom even in a thief—a common theme in Egyptian wisdom literature—clearly reflects its Egyptian origin. The translation is that of George Rawlinson, revised.

King Rhampsinitus possessed, they said, such great riches in silver that none of the kings who were his successors surpassed or even equaled his wealth. To better protect his treasure, he decided to build a stone building, one of whose walls abutted on the outer

wall of his palace. But the builder, who had designs upon the treasures, devised the following scheme. He arranged that one of the
stones in the wall could easily be removed from its place by two
men, or even by one. So the building was finished, and the king's
money stored away in it. Time passed, and when the builder was
near death, he called for his two sons, and told them that he had
taken care that they might live prosperously as a result of a con-
trivance he had made in the king's treasury. Then he gave them
clear directions about how to remove the stone, and told them its
measurements, and said that if they carefully kept the secret, they
would be stewards of the royal treasure. Then the father died, and
the sons quickly set to work. They went at night to the palace, found
the stone in the wall of the building, and after easily removing it,
took away much of the treasure.

When the king next opened the chamber, he was astonished to
see that the vessels were short of treasure. He did not know whom
to accuse, however, since the seals were all intact and the room
securely locked. Still, when he had opened the room a second and
a third time, he found that more money was gone, for the thieves
never stopped plundering the treasury. Finally, the king devised the
following plan. He ordered traps made, and set near the vessels
which contained his treasure. When the thieves came, as before,
and one of them entered and approached the jar, he was suddenly
caught in one of the traps. Realizing that he was lost, he instantly
called his brother, told him what had happened, and begged him to
enter as quickly as possible and cut off his head, lest by being seen
and recognized he should destroy his brother also. The other thief
thought the advice good, and was persuaded to follow it. Then, after
fitting the stone into its place, he went home, taking with him his
brother's head.

The next day, the king came into the room and was amazed to
see the headless body of the thief in the trap, while the building was
still whole, and neither entrance nor exit was to be seen anywhere.
Being at a loss, he devised the following plan. He ordered the body
of the dead man to be hung from the wall, and set guards to watch
it, with orders that if anyone was seen weeping or lamenting, that

person was to be seized and brought to him. Their mother suffered greatly because of the exposure of the corpse of her son. So she spoke to her surviving son, urging him to plan some way to free the body and bring it home. If he ignored what she said, she threatened that she would go herself to the king, and denounce him as having the treasure.

As the mother was furious with her surviving son, and he was unable to dissuade her, although he tried hard, he made the following plan. He readied some donkeys and loaded them with skins that he had filled with wine. Then he drove them before him until he came to the place where the guards were watching the dead body. Then he seized two or three of the skins and untied their necks. As the wine poured out, he began to beat his head and loudly shout, as though not knowing which of the donkeys he should turn to first. When the guards saw the wine pouring out freely, they rushed into the road with jars, hoping to profit from the accident by collecting the wine as it poured out. The driver pretended to be angry and loaded them all with abuse. Then, as the guards tried to console him, he pretended to gradually calm down and recover his good humor. Finally, he drove his asses aside out of the road and began rearranging their loads. As he talked and chatted with the guards, one of them began to tease him and make him laugh. At that he gave them one of the skins as a gift. Then they decided to sit down and have a drinking-party where they were, and they begged him to stay and drink with them. He let himself be persuaded, and stayed. As the drinking went on, they grew very friendly together, so presently he gave them another skin. They drank so freely that they became drunk, and, growing sleepy, lay down, and fell asleep right where they were drinking. The thief waited through most of the night, and then took down the body of his brother. Then, to mock the guards, he shaved off the right side of all their faces. Loading his brother's body upon the asses, he carried it home, having accomplished what his mother had demanded of him.

When the king learned that the thief's body had been stolen away, he was outraged. Wishing at all cost to discover the man who had contrived he trick, he did something, they say, which I cannot believe. He placed his daughter in a room, with orders to admit all comers, but to require every man before having intercourse with her to tell her what was the cleverest and wickedest thing he had done during his life. If anyone told her the story of the thief, she was to seize him and not allow him to go away. The daughter followed her father's instructions, and the thief, who understood the purpose of these measures and desired to outwit the king, did the following. He cut off at the shoulder one of the arms of the corpse of a man who had recently died, put it under his cloak, and went to the king's daughter. When she asked him the same question she had asked all the other men, he replied that the wickedest thing he had ever done was cutting off the head of his brother when he was caught in a trap in the King's treasury, and the cleverest was making the guards drunk and taking down the hanging body of his brother. When she heard this, the princess tried to grab him, but the thief in the darkness held out to her the hand of the corpse. She took hold of it, thinking that she had had hold of his hand. Meanwhile the thief, leaving it in her grasp, escaped through the door.

When these things were reported to the king, he was amazed at the cleverness and daring of the man, and finally sent messengers to every city to proclaim a free pardon for the thief, and to promise him a rich reward, if he came into his presence. The thief trusted the king's word and came to him; and Rhampsinitus admired him greatly and married his daughter to him on the ground that he was the wisest of all men. For the Egyptians were superior to all other men and he to all other Egyptians.

GRECO-ROMAN EGYPT

The Miracles of Khonsu

Besides entertainment and edification, fiction could also be used in ancient Egypt for religious propaganda. A good example is this story of the miraculous victories of the Theban god Khonsu over a powerful demon and a scheming prince.[1] Although writing sometime in the second half of the first millennium B.C.E., its pious author used the physical and literary form of a royal decree and included real incidents from the reign of the great Nineteenth Dynasty king Ramses II (1279–1212 B.C.E.)—his marriage to a Hittite princess—in order to enhance of the credibility of his tale. The only source for this story is a monumental stele preserved in the Louvre.

Horus: Mighty bull, beautiful of crowns; Two Ladies: Abiding in kingship like Atum; Golden Horus: Strong-armed smiter of the Nine Bows; the King of Upper and Lower Egypt. Lord of the Two Lands: Usermare-sotpenre; the Son of Re, of his body: Ramesse

---

1. Translated by Miriam Lichtheim, *Ancient Egyptian Literature*, vol. 3: *The Late Period* (Berkeley and Los Angeles: University of California Press, 1980), pp. 91–93. Copyright © 1980 by the Regents of the University of California; used by permission.

beloved of Amun, beloved of Amen-Re, lord of Thrones-of-the-Two-Lands, and of the Ennead, mistress of Thebes.[2]

> Good god, Amun's son,
> Offspring of Harakhti,
> Glorious seed of the All-Lord,
> Begotten by Kamutef,
> King of Egypt, ruler of Red Lands,
> Sovereign who seized the Nine Bows;
> Whom victory was foretold as he came from the womb,
> Whom valor was given while in the egg,
> Bull firm of heart as he treads the arena,
> Godly king going forth like Mont on victory day,
> Great of strength like the Son of Nut!

When his majesty was in Nahrin[3] acording to his annual custom, the princes of every foreign land came bowing in peace to the might of his majesty from as far as the farthest marshlands. Their gifts of gold, silver, lapis lazuli, turquoise, and every kind of plant of god's land were on their backs, and each was outdoing his fellow. The prince of Bakhtan had also sent his gifts and had placed his eldest daughter in front of them, worshipping his majesty and begging life from him. The woman pleased the heart of his majesty greatly and beyond anything. So her titulary was established as Great Royal Wife Nefrure.[4] When his majesty returned to Egypt, she did all that a queen does.

It happened in year 23, second month of summer, day 22, while his majesty was in Thebes-the-victorious, the mistress of cities, performing the rites for his father Amen-Re, lord of Thrones-of-the-Two-Lands, at his beautiful feast of Sourthern Ipet, his favorite place since the beginning, that one came to say to his majesty:

---

2. That the author aimed for historical plausibility and not exactitude is indicated by the royal titulary which mixes elements of the titularies of Ramses II and the Eighteenth Dynasty king Tuthmosis IV (1401–1390 B.C.E.).

3. The Egyptian term for the kingdom of Mittani in northern Mesopotamia, which was one of Egypt's principal allies during the New Kingdom.

4. The queen's name echoes that of Ramses II's Hittite wife, Maatnefrure.

"A messenger of the prince of Bakhtan[5] has come with many gifts for the queen." He was brought before his majesty with his gifts and said, saluting his majesty: "Hail to you, Sun of the Nine Bows! Truly, we live through you!" And kissing the ground before his majesty, he spoke again before his majesty, saying: "I have come to you, O King, my lord, on account of Bentresh, the younger sister of Queen Nefrure. A malady has seized her body. May your majesty send a learned man to see her!"

His majesty said: "Bring me the personnel of the House of Life and the council of the residence." They were ushered in to him immediately. His majesty said: "You have been summoned in order to hear this matter: bring me one wise of heart with fingers skilled in writing from among you." Then the royal scribe Thothemheb came before his majesty, and his majesty ordered him to proceed to Bakhtan with the messenger.

The learned man reached Bakhtan. He found Bentresh to be possessed by a spirit; he found him to be an enemy whom one could fight. Then the prince of Bakhtan sent again to his majesty, saying: "O King, my lord, may your majesty command to send a god [to fight against this spirit!" The message reached] his majesty in year 26, first month of summer, during the feast of Amun while his majesty was in Thebes. His majesty reported to Khons-in-Thebes-Neferhotep,[6] saying: "My good lord, I report to you about the daughter of the prince of Bakhtan." Then Khons-in-Thebes-Neferhotep proceeded to Khons-the-Provider, the great god who expels disease demons. His majesty spoke to Khons-in-Thebes-Neferhotep: "My good lord, if you turn your face to Khons-the-Provider, the great god who expels disease demons, he shall be dispatched to Bakhtan." Strong approval twice.[7] His majesty said: "Give your

---

5.The location of Bakhtan is unclear. It is usually explained as a corruption of the term for Bactria, modern Afghanistan, although a strong case has been made recently that the tale's author misread the New Kingdom writing of Hatti, the land of the Hittites (cf. A. Spalinger, *JSSEA Journal* 8 [1977]: 11–18), which would fit better with the historical background of the story.

6. The principal form of the Theban moon god Khonsu, who was believed to be the son of Amun and the goddess Mut.

7. The god's statue indicates its approval of the proposal by nodding twice.

magical protection to him, and I shall dispatch his majesty to Bakhtan to save the daughter of the prince of Bakhtan." Very strong approval by Khons-in-Thebes-Neferhotep. He made magical protection for Khons-the-Provider-in-Thebes four times. His majesty commanded to let Khons-the-Provider-in-Thebes proceed to the great bark with five boats and a chariot, and many horses from east and west.

This god arrived in Bakhtan at the end of one year and five months. The prince of Bakhtan came with his soldiers and officials before the Khons-the-Provider. He placed himself on his belly, saying: "You have come to us to be gracious to us, as commanded by the King of Upper and Lower Egypt, Usermare-sotpenre!" Then the god proceeded to the place where Bentresh was. He made magical protection for the daughter of the prince of Bakhtan, and she became well instantly.

Then spoke the spirit who was with her to Khons-the-Provider-in-Thebes: "Welcome in peace, great god who expels disease demons! Bakhtan is your home, its people are your servants, I am your servant! I shall go to the place from which I came, so as to set your heart at rest about that for which you came. May your majesty command to make a feast day with me and the prince of Bakhtan!" Then the god motioned approval to his priest, saying: "Let the prince of Bakhtan make a great offering before this spirit."

Now while this took place between Khons-the-Provider-in-Thebes and the spirit, the prince of Bakhtan stood by with his soldiers and was very frightened. Then he made a great offering to Khons-the-Provider-in-Thebes and the spirit; and the prince of Bakhtan made a feast day for them. Then the spirit went in peace to where he wished, as commanded by Khons-the-Provider-in-Thebes. The prince of Bakhtan rejoiced very greatly together with everyone in Bakhtan.

Then he schemed with his heart, saying: "I will make the god stay here in Bakhtan. I will not let him go to Egypt." So the god spent three years and nine months in Bakhtan. Then, as the prince of Bakhtan slept on his bed, he saw the god come out of his shrine as a falcon of gold[8] and fly up to the sky toward Egypt. He awoke in terror and said to the priest of Khons-the-Provider-in-Thebes: "The god is still here with us! He shall go to Thebes! His chariot shall go to Egypt!" Then the prince of Bakhtan let the god proceed to Egypt, having given him many gifts of every good thing and very many soldiers and horses.

They arrived in peace in Thebes. Khons-the-Provider-in-Thebes went to the house of Khons-in-Thebes-Neferhotep. He placed the gifts of every good thing which the prince of Bakhtan had given him before Khons-in-Thebes-Neferhotep, without giving anything to his [own] house. Khons-the-Provider-in-Thebes arrived in his house in peace in year 33, second month of winter, day 19, of the King of Upper and Lower Egypt, Usermare-sotpenre, given eternal life like Re.

---

8. The flesh of gods was supposed to be made of gold.

The Story of Khamwise

This is chiefly known to us from an incomplete manuscript on papyrus, said to have been found at Thebes, and now in the Cairo Museum; it is of the Ptolemaic Period, probably the third century B.C.E., and is in Demotic writing. It had originally six numbered pages, but the first two, and with them the beginnings[1] of the lines of the third page, have been torn away and lost. A fragment of this story or a closely related one also exists; it may have belonged to the missing part of the story in another manuscript, but since it does not yield any connected narrative it has not been used here.

The hero of the story is a historical figure: Prince Khamwise, one of the elder, and the most notable, of the 111 + x sons of the great King Ramses II. Early in life he took a prominent part in his father's campaigns in Syria and Nubia. Later he was appointed to one of the very highest ecclesiastical offices in the country, the Chief Priesthood of the Memphite god Ptah, which carried with it the title of "setom"-priest (a very old title of unknown meaning), by which he was generally known to posterity. He seems to have been one of the favorite sons of the King, who made him his representative

---

1. These beginnings have been restored in the translation; in many cases the restoration is certain.

in many religious and State ceremonies from about the thirtieth year of his reign. Khamwise manifested a great devotion to the cult of the sacred Apis-bulls of Memphis, and was apparently responsible for the construction of part of the Apis-catacombs at Sakkarah known as the Serapeum, where records of him have been found. He died some twelve years before his father, who reigned sixty-seven years (about 1279–1212 B.C.E.), and must have been nearly, if not quite, 100 at his death. We have many material remains of the Setom: his tomb near the Great Pyramid, his mummy at Cairo, a good statue in the British Museum, and many records and small objects connected with him, including a letter to him in which report is made about some of his servants. There was a tradition that he discovered a potent magic spell "by the head of a mummy on the west of Memphis (Sakkarah)," and in still later times he had, as we shall see, the reputation of an enthusiast for magic. There is no contemporary evidence of the occurrence of any of the events, or of the existence of persons other than the Setom and his father, mentioned in the story, the missing part of which may be reconstructed in skeleton form somewhat as follows:

Khamwise, son of Pharaoh Usimare Ramses (the second), and Chief Priest and Setom of Ptah, was "a good scribe" (i.e. a magician) and a very learned man, and a lover of ancient writings. It befell that he learned of the existence of a wonderful book of magic which Thoth (the god of wisdom and learning) had written with his own hand, and which was in the tomb of a certain Prince Neferkaptah (son of Pharaoh Merneptah), who had lived a long time previously and was buried in the vast cemetery of Memphis. Khamwise having by some means found this tomb, entered it, accompanied by his foster-brother Inharerow. There he found the ghost of Neferkaptah, and with him were the ghosts of his wife Ahwere and their child Meryeb, although these two were buried a great way off at Coptos. Between Neferkaptah and Ahwere was the book, which shed throughout the tomb a light as strong as that of the sun. Khamwise demanded the book; but they refused to give it to him, saying that they had paid for it with their lives. To discourage him from taking it, Ahwere told him their story, the lost beginning of which may be summarized thus:

"It happened in the time of my father, Pharaoh Merneptah, that Pharaoh grew old, and had no child but me and my elder brother Neferkaptah, who is beside me. Now Pharaoh greatly desired that there should be children of his children, and at a certain moment he commanded that a feast should be made before him after some days, and that the sons and the daughters of the generals should be invited, that Pharaoh might choose for me a husband from the sons of the generals and for my brother Neferkaptah a wife from the daughters of the generals, that the family might thereby be increased.

And a steward of Pharaoh's house, an aged man, whom Pharaoh loved, told us of Pharaoh's plan; and we became sad, and very much afraid, for we loved one another exceedingly. And I went to the steward and I said to him, 'Speak with Pharaoh, that he may marry Neferkaptah and me to one another, and not part us; for we love one another exceedingly.' And the steward of Pharaoh's house went before Pharaoh, and said before him, 'My great Lord—O may you live as long as the Sun-god!—is it not fitting that Pharaoh should follow the custom of his fathers and marry Neferkaptah to Ahwere, that children may be born in the family of Pharaoh? For Neferkaptah and Ahwere love one another exceedingly.' And Pharaoh was silent, and he was sad. The steward said before him, 'What is it that troubles my lord?' And Pharaoh said to the steward,

"'It is you who offend me. If it happens that I have only two children, is it the law to marry one of them to the other? I will marry Neferkaptah to the daughter of a general, and I will marry Ahwere to the son of another general, so that it comes about that our family increases.'"

"When the time came for the banquet to be set before Pharaoh, I was sent for and taken to that banquet. It happened that I was very sad, not being in my previous humor.

"Pharaoh said to me, 'Ahwere, was it you who sent to me with those foolish words, "Let me marry Neferkaptah, my elder brother"?'

"I said to him, 'Let me marry the son of a general, and let him marry the daughter of another general, so that it comes about that our family increases.' I laughed, and Pharaoh laughed, and he was very happy.

"Pharaoh said to the steward of the King's House, 'Let Ahwere be taken to Neferkaptah's house to-night, and let all sorts of beautiful things be taken with her.' I was taken as a wife to Neferkaptah's house on that same night. Pharaoh sent me a present of silver and gold, and all Pharaoh's household sent me presents. Neferkaptah made holiday with me, and he entertained all Pharaoh's household. He slept with me that night, and found me pleasing. He never quarreled with me; each of us did the other's wish.

"When my time of making purification came, I made no more purification. It was reported to Pharaoh, and he was very pleased.

He had many things taken out of the treasury for me, and sent me very beautiful presents of silver and gold and royal linen.

"When my time of bearing came, I bore this boy who is before you, and who was named Meryeb. He was sent to study writings in the House of Life.[2]

"It so happened that my brother Neferkaptah had no occupation on earth but walking in the cemetery of Memphis, reading the writings which were in the tombs of the Pharaohs, and on the tombstones[3] of the scribes of the House of Life, and the writings on the other monuments, for his zeal concerning writings was very great.

"After these things there was a procession in honor of the god Ptah, and Neferkaptah went into the temple to worship. It happened, while he was walking behind the procession, reading the writings on the shrines of the gods, that an old priest saw him, and laughed.

"Neferkaptah said to him, 'Why are you laughing at me?'

"He said, 'I am not laughing at you; I am laughing because you are reading writings which have no importance to any man on earth. If you wish to read writings, come to me that I may have you taken to the place where that book is that Thoth wrote with his own hand when he went down following the other gods.[4] What it contains is two written spells. Reciting the first spell, you will enchant the sky, the earth, the underworld, the hills and the waters. You will find out what all the birds of the sky and the creeping things are saying. You will see the fish of the river, with a Divine Power[5] resting in the water over them. Reciting the second spell, whether you are in Amenti[6] or again on earth in your usual form, you will see the Sun-god shining in the sky with his Nine Gods, and the Moon in its form of rising.'

---

2. A place where religious and magical works, and probably some other formal texts (see next paragraph), were composed. There Meryeb was put to learn hieroglyphic writing.

3. Probably these did not belong to, but bore inscriptions composed by, the scribes in question.

4. Obscure.

5. An obscure entity, resting in the water over fish and drowned persons, which is mentioned several times in the story.

6. The "west," home of the dead.

"Neferkaptah said to him, 'As you live, please tell me any good thing that you wish for, that I may have it done for you, if you will send me to the place where this book is!'

"The priest said to Neferkaptah, 'If you wish to be sent to the place where this book is, you must give me twenty pounds' weight of silver for my burial, and you must endow me with two priestly stipends, without curtailment.'

"Neferkaptah called a servant, and had the twenty pounds' weight of silver given to the priest; he added the two stipends, and had the priest endowed with them without curtailment.

"The priest said to Neferkaptah, 'The book in question is in the middle of the water of Coptos[7] in an iron box; in the iron box is a bronze box; in the bronze box is a box of juniper-wood; in the box of juniper-wood is an ivory and ebony[8] box; in the ivory and ebony box is a silver box; in the silver box is a golden box, in which is the book. There are two leagues[9] of serpents and scorpions and all manner of creeping things around the box that the book is in; and there is an eternal serpent around this same box.'

"When the priest had spoken to Neferkaptah he did not know where on earth he was.[10] He came out of the temple, he told me everything that had happened to him. He said to me, 'I will go to Coptos and bring back this book, hastening back to the north again.'

"It happened that I reproached the priest, saying, 'May Neith[11] curse you! Why have you told him these baleful things? You have caused me fighting, you have brought me contention. I have found the Theban country cruel.'[12]

"I did what I could with Neferkaptah to prevent him from going to Coptos; he did not listen to me. He went before Pharaoh, and

---

7. A large town about twenty-five miles north of Thebes, and the capital of a county. "The water [literally, sea] of Coptos" is an obscure term, unknown outside this story.
8. That is, ebony inlaid with ivory; so also of the bed mentioned near the end of the story.
9. Really a single measure of length equal to about six-and-a-half miles.
10. An expression for extreme wonder or delight.
11. A goddess of northern Egypt, worshipped especially at Sais.
12. The relevance of this remark is obscure.

related before him everything that the priest had told him. Pharaoh said to him, 'What is it that you want?' He said to him, 'Let the royal barge and its equipment be given to me; I will take Ahwere and her boy Meryeb to the south with me, and bring back this book without delay.'

"The royal barge and its equipment were given to him. We went on board it, we set sail, and reached Coptos. It was announced to the priests of Isis of Coptos and the chief priest of Isis. They came down to meet us; they hastened to meet Neferkaptah, and their wives came down to meet me. We went up from the shore, and went into the temple of Isis and Harpocrates.[13] Neferkaptah sent for an ox, a goose and wine; he made burnt offering and libation before Isis of Coptos and Harpocrates. We were taken to a very beautiful house, filled with all good things.

"Neferkaptah spent four days making holiday with the priests of Isis of Coptos, and the wives of the priests of Isis made holiday with me. When the morning of our fifth day came, Neferkaptah had much pure wax brought to him, and made a boat, filled with its rowers and sailors; he recited a spell to them, and made them come to life, and gave them breath, and put them on the water. He filled the royal barge with sand, and tied it to the other boat. He went on board, and I myself sat over against the water of Coptos, saying, 'I will find out what becomes of him.'

"He said to the rowers, 'Row me to the place where that book is.' They rowed him by night as by day. Then he reached it, in three days. He cast sand in front of him, and a gap formed in the river. Then he found two leagues of serpents and scorpions and all manner of creeping things around the place where the book was. Then he found an eternal serpent around this same box. He recited a spell to the two leagues of snakes and scorpions and all kinds of creeping things which were around the box, and stopped them from coming up. He went to the place where the eternal serpent was; he fought it and killed it; it came to life and recovered its nature. He fought it again, a second time, and killed it; it came to life

---

13. Har-pe-khrat, "Horus the child."

again. He fought it again, a third time; he cut it into two pieces, and put sand between one piece and the other; it died, and never recovered its nature.

"Neferkaptah went to the place where the box was. He found that it was an iron box; he opened it and found a bronze box; he opened it and found a box of juniper-wood; he opened it and found an ivory and ebony box; he opened it and found a silver box; he opened it and found a golden box; he opened it and found the book in it. He brought the book up out of the golden box.

"He recited a spell from it; he enchanted the sky, the earth, the underworld, the hills and the waters; he found out what all the birds of the sky and the fish of the river and the beasts of the desert were saying. He recited another spell; he saw the Sun-god shining in the sky with his Nine Gods, and the Moon rising, and the stars in their [true] forms; he saw the fish of the river, with Divine Power resting in the water over them. He recited a spell to the water, and made it recover its form.

"He went on board, and said to the rowers, 'Row me back to the place I came from.' They rowed him by night as by day. Then he reached me, at the place where I was; he found me sitting over against the water of Coptos, not having drunk nor eaten, not having done everything on earth, and looking like a person who has reached the Good House.[14]

"I said to Neferkaptah, 'Welcome back! Let me see this book for which we have taken these great pains.' He put the book into my hand. I recited one spell from it; I enchanted the sky, the earth, the underworld, the hills and the waters. I found out what all the birds of the sky, the fish of the river and the beasts were saying. I recited another spell; I saw the Sun-god shining in the sky with his Nine Gods; I saw the Moon rising, and all the stars of the sky with their [true] forms; I saw the fish of the river, with Divine Power resting in the water over them.

"As I could not write I was speaking to[15] Neferkaptah, my elder

---

14. The workshop in which corpses were embalmed and wrapped.
15. This is quite obscure to me.

brother, who was a good scribe and a very wise man. He had a sheet of new papyrus brought to him, and he wrote on it every word that was in the book before him; he burned it,[16] and dissolved the ashes in water; when he knew that it had dissolved he drank it[17] and knew what had been in it.

"We returned to Coptos the same day, and made holiday before Isis of Coptos and Harpocrates. We went on board, we traveled downstream, we reached a point two leagues north of Coptos.

"Now Thoth had already found out everything that had happened to Neferkaptah regarding the book. Thoth hastened to announce it before the Sun-god, saying, 'Ascertain my right and my cause with Neferkaptah the son of Pharaoh Merneptah! He went to my treasury, he plundered it, and carried off my chest with my documents; he killed my guardian who was watching over it.' He was told, 'He and every person belonging to him are at your disposal.' They sent a Power of God down from heaven, saying, 'Do not allow Neferkaptah or any person belonging to him to get to Memphis in safety.'

"At a certain moment the boy Meryeb came out from under the awning of the royal barge, and fell into the river, and was drowned. Everyone on board uttered a cry. Neferkaptah came out from his tent, he recited a spell to him, and made him rise up, with a Divine Power resting in the water over him. He recited a spell to him, and made him relate to him everything that had happened to him, and the manner of accusation that Thoth had made before the Sun-god.

"We went back to Coptos with him, and had him taken to the Good House; we had him tended, and embalmed like a prince, an important person; and we laid him to rest in his stone coffin in the cemetery of Coptos.

"Neferkaptah, my brother, said, 'Let us go north. Let us hasten, lest Pharaoh hear the things that have happened to us, and grow sad because of them.' We went on board, we went north, we made haste.

---

16. That is, the copy.
17. Similar methods of absorbing knowledge or magical powers are and have been widespread in the East.

"Two leagues north of Coptos, at the place where the boy Mer-yeb had fallen into the river, I came out from under the awning of the royal barge, and fell into the river, and was drowned. Everyone on board uttered a cry. They told Neferkaptah, who came out from the tent of the royal barge; he recited a spell to me, and made me rise up, with a Divine Power resting in the water over me. He had me brought up, and recited a spell to me, and made me relate to him everything that had happened to me, and the manner of accu-sation that Thoth had made before the Sun-god.

"He went back to Coptos with me, and had me taken to the Good House; he had me tended, and embalmed as befits a prince, a very important person, and laid me to rest in the tomb in which the boy Meryeb was resting. He went on board, he went north, he made haste.

"Two leagues north of Coptos, at the place where we had fallen into the river, he spoke with his heart, saying, 'Can I go to Coptos and dwell there? Otherwise, if I go to Memphis now, and Pharaoh questions me about his children, what shall I say to him? Can I tell him, "I took your children to the county of Thebes, and killed them, I living on; and I have come to Memphis still alive"?'

"He sent for a strip of royal linen belonging to him, and made it into a bandage; he bound the book round, and put it on his body, and made it fast. Neferkaptah came out from under the awning of the royal barge, and fell into the river, and was drowned. Everyone on board uttered a cry, saying, 'Great woe, grievous woe! Will he return, the good scribe, the learned man whose like has not been?'

"The royal barge sailed on northwards, no man on earth know-ing where Neferkaptah was. They reached Memphis; it was an-nounced before Pharaoh. Pharaoh came down to meet the royal barge, in mourning garments, and all the people of Memphis were wearing mourning, and the priests of Ptah, the chief priest of Ptah, and the Council, and Pharaoh's household, all of them. Then they saw Neferkaptah grasping the rudders[18] of the royal barge through his craft of a good scribe. They brought him up, they saw the book

---

18. An Egyptian boat had two, oar-shaped.

on his body.

"Pharaoh said, 'Let this book which is on his body be hidden away.' The Council of Pharaoh, and the priests of Ptah, and the chief priest of Ptah, said before Pharaoh, 'Our great lord—O may you live as long as the Sun-god—Neferkaptah was a good scribe and a very learned man.'

"Pharaoh made them give him entry to the Good House on the sixteenth day, wrapping on the thirty-fifth, burial on the seventieth day;[19] and they laid him to rest in his stone coffin in his resting-places.

"Behold the evil things which happened to us on account of this book of which you say, 'Let it be given to me.' You have no claim to it, while our lives were cut off on earth because of it."[20]

The Setom said to Ahwere, "Let me have this book which I saw between you and Neferkaptah, or else I will take it by force."

Neferkaptah arose from the bier and said, "You, Setom, to whom this woman is telling these dire things, which you have not suffered at all, will you be able to seize the book in question through the power of a good scribe, or skill in playing draughts with me? Let the two of us play draughts for it." The Setom said, "I am ready."

The draught-board and its pieces were set before them, and they both played. Neferkaptah won one game from the Setom; Neferkaptah recited a spell to him, he struck his head with the draught-box before him, and made him sink into the ground as far as his feet. He did the same with the second game; he won it from the Setom, and made him sink into the ground as far as his middle. He did the same with the third game, and made him sink into the ground as far as his ears. After this the Setom suffered great straits at the hands of Neferkaptah. The Setom called out to Inharerow, his foster-brother, saying, "Hasten up on to the earth, and relate before

---

19. These were the chief points in the complex treatment of the dead, which included evisceration, pickling the body in a salt-water tank, impregnating with unguents and spices, and elaborate wrapping with clothes and bandages.

20. Here ends Ahwere's long narrative, and here the Setom Khamwise, to whom Ahwere has been speaking, first appears in the extant part of the manuscript.

Pharaoh everything that has happened to me; and bring the talismans of my father[21] Ptah, and my books of sorcery."

He hastened up on to the earth, and related before Pharaoh everything that had happened to the Setom. Pharaoh said, "Take him the talismans of his father Ptah, and his books of sorcery." Inharerow hastened down into the tomb; he put the talismans on the body of the Setom, who instantly sprang upwards. The Setom reached out for the book, and took it away. And it befell that he came up out of the tomb, the light going before him,[22] the darkness going behind him, Ahwere weeping for it and saying, "Hail, O darkness! Farewell, O light! Everything that was in the tomb has departed." Neferkaptah said to Ahwere, "Do not be sad; I will make him bring this book back here, with a forked stick in his hand, and a lighted brazier on his head."[23]

The Setom came up out of the tomb, and made it fast behind him, as it had been. He went before Pharaoh, and related before him everything that had happened to him through the book. Pharaoh said to the Setom, "Take this book back to Neferkaptah's tomb like a wise man, or else he will make you return it with a forked stick in your hand, and a lighted brazier on your head." The Setom did not listen to him, and it came about that he had no occupation on earth but to unroll the book and read from it to everyone.

After these things it happened one day that the Setom was strolling about in the forecourt of the temple of Ptah. Then he saw a very beautiful woman. No other woman had been so splendid: she was beautiful,[24] and wore many golden jewels, with some female attendants walking behind her, there being two men, like domestics, belonging to her.

---

21. That this son of Ramses II should refer to Ptah, whose chief priest he was, as his father is highly abnormal.

22. The magic book radiates light; see the description of its return to the tomb, p. 00 (later in this story).

23. The significance of the forked stick and burning brazier (mentioned several times later) is obscure, except that they seem to express humility or repentance. A burning brazier as a signal of capitulation of a foreign city is known from battle-scenes.

24. The sense is probably: "not only was she beautiful (as already mentioned), but also she wore, etc."

The moment that the Setom saw her, he did not know where on earth he was. He called his page, saying, "Hasten to where that woman is, and find out how it stands with her position." The page hastened to where the woman was, he addressed the serving-girl who was following her, and asked her, "What person is this?" She told him, "She is Tabubu, the daughter of the prophet of Obaste[25] Mistress of Anekhtowe;[26] she has come here to worship the great god Ptah."[27]

The boy returned to the Setom, and reported to him every word that she had said to him. The Setom said to the boy, "Go, say to the girl,[28] 'It is the Setom, Khamwise, the son of Pharaoh Usimare, who has sent me, saying, "I will give you ten pieces of gold—spend an hour with me. Or have you an accusation of injury? I will have it settled for you. I will have you taken to a hidden place where no one on earth shall find you."'"

The boy went back to where Tabubu was, he called to her serving-maid, and told her; she made an outcry as though what he had said was blasphemy. Tabubu said to the boy, "Stop arguing with this fool of a girl, come and speak with me."

The boy ran to where Tabubu was, and said to her, "I will give you ten pieces of gold; spend an hour with the Setom, Khamwise, the son of Pharaoh Usimare. Have you an accusation of injury? He will have it settled, too. He will take you to a hidden place where no one on earth shall find you."

Tabubu said, "Go, tell the Setom, 'I am of priestly rank, I am not a low person. If you want to do what you wish with me you must come to Pubaste, to my house; everything is ready in it, and you shall do what you wish with me, no one on earth having discovered me, and I not having acted as a low woman of the streets.'"

The boy went back to the Setom, and related to him everything that she had said to him. He said, "That's all right." Everyone about the Setom was shocked.

---

25. An important cat goddess, worshipped chiefly at Pubáste or Bubastis ("House of Ubáste"), a city of northern Egypt, mentioned below.

26. A district or suburb of Memphis where Ubáste was worshipped.

27. Tabubu is thought by some to be a magical projection of Ahwere.

28. As a message to Tabubu.

The Setom had a traveling-boat brought to him; he went on board it, he hastened to Pubaste, and came to the west of the town. Then he found a very lofty house, having an enclosure-wall round it, a garden being on its north, and a terrace at its door. The Setom asked, "Whose house is this?" They told him, "It is Tabubu's house." He went inside the wall; then he turned his attention to the garden store-house while they announced his arrival to Tabubu. She came down, and grasped the Setom's hand, and said to him, "By the prosperity of the house of the Prophet of Ubaste Mistress of Anekhtowe, which you have reached, it will please me greatly if you give yourself the trouble to come up with me."

The Setom walked upstairs with Tabubu. And he found the upper part of the house cleaned and garnished, its ceiling being decorated with real lapis lazuli and real turquoise, many couches being in it spread with royal linen, and many golden cups being on the dining table. A golden cup was filled with wine and given into the Setom's hand. Tabubu said, "Be pleased to eat something"; he said, "I could not do so." Incense was put on the brazier; unguent was brought to him, of the kind provided for Pharaoh. The Setom made holiday with Tabubu; he had never seen her like at all.

He said to Tabubu, "Let us do what we have come here for." She said to him, "You will return to your house in which you live; I am of priestly rank, I am not a low person. If you want to do what you wish with me you must make me a deed of maintenance and one for money regarding everything, all goods, belonging to you."[29] He said to her, "Send for the schoolmaster."[30] He was brought at once. The Setom had made for her a deed of maintenance and compensation in money regarding everything, all goods, belonging to him.

At a certain moment it was announced to the Setom, "Your children are below." He said, "Let them be brought up." Tabubu arose, she put on a garment of royal linen,[31] and the Setom saw every part of her through it. Then his desire became greater than it had been

---

29. Egyptian marriage settlements contained provision for the wife's maintenance, and for inheritance by the children, together with an undertaking to reimburse the wife for her dowry and property brought in by her if the parties separate.

30. One of whose functions is still, in Egypt, to draw up marriage-settlements.

31. Noted for its extreme fineness.

before. He said to Tabubu, "Let me do what I have come here for."

She said to him, "You will return to your house in which you live; I am of priestly rank, I am not a low person. If you want to do what you wish with me, you must make your children subscribe my deed; do not leave them to contend with my children over your property." He had his children fetched; he made them subscribe the deed.

The Setom said to Tabubu, "Let me do what I have come here for." She said to him, "You will return to your house in which you live; I am of priestly rank, I am not a low person. If you want to do what you wish with me, you must have your children killed; do not leave them to contend with my children over your property." The Setom said, "Let the abomination that you think fitting be done to them." She had his children killed before him, she had them thrown down from the window before the dogs and cats;[32] they ate their flesh, while the Setom heard them, drinking with Tabubu.

The Setom said to Tabubu, "Let us do what we have come here for. All the things that you have said, I have done them all for you." She said to him, "Please move to this strong-room."

The Setom went to the strong-room; he lay down on an ivory and ebony bed, his desire about to be fulfilled. Tabubu lay down beside him. He reached out his hand to touch her, and she opened her mouth wide in a great cry. Then the Setom awoke, being in a state of great heat, et cetera, with no clothes on him at all.

At a certain moment he saw an important man[33] riding in a chariot, with many men running beside him, he being like a Pharaoh. The Setom tried to rise; he could not rise for shame, because he had no clothes on.

The Pharaoh said, "Setom, why are you in this state that you are in?" He said, "It is Neferkaptah who has done it all to me."

The Pharaoh said, "Go to Memphis, and your children; they want you, they are standing up before Pharaoh." The Setom said to the Pharaoh, "My great lord,—O may you live as long as the Sun-

---

32. Egyptian cats are much fiercer than European ones.
33. Thought by some to be Neferkaptah in magic disguise.

god!—how can I go to Memphis, with no clothes on me at all?"

The Pharaoh called to a servant who was standing by, and made him give clothes to the Setom. The Pharaoh said, "Setom, go to Memphis and your children; they are alive, and standing up before Pharaoh."

The Setom went to Memphis; he embraced his children, when he found them alive. Pharaoh said, "Is it drunk you were before?" The Setom related everything that had happened to him and Tabubu and Neferkaptah, all of them.

Pharaoh said, "Setom, I did what I could with you formerly, saying, 'They will kill you if you do not take this book back to the place where you took it away,' and you have not listed to me until now. Take this book back to Neferkaptah, with a forked stick in your hand and a lighted brazier on your head."

The Setom came out from before Pharaoh, with a forked stick in his hand and a lighted brazier on his head; he went down to the tomb that Neferkaptah was in.

Ahwere said to him, "Setom, it is the great god Ptah who has brought you back safely." Neferkaptah laughed, saying, "It's what I told you before." The Setom greeted Neferkaptah, he found one would have said it was the Sun-god who was in the whole tomb.[34] Ahwere and Neferkaptah greeted the Setom fervently.

The Setom said, "Neferkaptah, is there any matter which is shameful?" Neferkaptah said, "Setom, you know that Ahwere and her son Meryeb are in Coptos, and also here in this tomb, by the craft of a good scribe. Let it be demanded of you to undertake a task, and to go to Coptos and bring them here."

The Setom came up out of the tomb; he went before Pharaoh, and related before him everything Neferkaptah had said to him. Pharaoh said, "Setom, go to Coptos, bring Ahwere and her son Meryeb." He said to Pharaoh, "Let the royal barge and its equipment be given to me."

The royal barge and its equipment were given to him; he went on board, and set sail, and hastened, and reached Coptos. It was

---

34. The magic book shone so brightly.

announced to the priests of Isis of Coptos, and the chief priest of Isis. They came down to meet him, they took his hand to the shore.

He went up from it, and went into the temple of Isis of Coptos and Harpocrates. He sent for an ox and a goose, and wine, he made burnt-offering and libation before Isis of Coptos and Harpocrates. He went to the cemetery of Coptos with the priests of Isis and the chief priest of Isis; they spent three days and nights searching in all the tombs in the cemetery of Coptos, turning over the tombstones[35] of the scribes of the House of Life, and reading the inscriptions on them, but they did not find the resting-places in which Ahwere and her son Meryeb were.

Neferkaptah found that they had not found the resting-places of Ahwere and her son Meryeb. He rose up as an old man, a very aged priest; he came to meet the Setom.

The Setom saw him, and said to the old man, "You have the appearance of an aged man. Do you know the resting-places in which Ahwere and her son Meryeb are?" The old man said to him, "My great-grandfather said to my grandfather, 'My great-grandfather said to my grandfather, "The resting-places of Ahwere and her son Meryeb are by the south corner of the house of the chief of police."'"

The Setom said to the old man, "Perhaps there is some injustice that the chief of police did you, because of which you are trying to get his house pulled down." The old man said to him, "Have a watch set over me, and let the house of the chief of police be demolished; if they then have not found Ahwere and her son Meryeb under the south corner of his house let some abominable thing be done to me."

They set a watch over the old man, and they found the resting-place of Ahwere and her son Meryeb under the south corner of the house of the chief of police. The Setom gave the two important persons entry into the royal barge, and had the house of the chief of police rebuilt as it had been formerly.

---

35. Many of these had evidently fallen down on their faces. And see p. 81, note 3.

Neferkaptah let the Setom find out the fact that it was he who had come to Coptos to enable the resting-place containing Ahwere and her son Meryeb to be found. The Setom went on board the royal barge, he went north, he hastened and reached Memphis with all the people who were with him.

It was announced before Pharaoh; he came down to meet the royal barge. He gave the important people entry to the tomb that Neferkaptah was in, he had it filled in over them, all together.

This story of the Setom Khamwise and Neferkaptah and his wife Ahwere and her son Meryeb is a complete writing. The "god's-father"[36] *Tjehorpeto copied it. Year 15, first winter month.*

---

36. An obscure priestly title.

The Dream of Nectanebo

Although only the beginning survives of "The Dream of Nectanebo," this brief text is one of the most important surviving examples of Hellenistic Egyptian fiction. Discovered in the early nineteenth century among the papers of a Macedonian named Apollonius, who was living in the Serapeum at Memphis, "The Dream of Nectanebo" was immediately recognized as a Greek translation of an Egyptian story[1]—fragments of the Egyptian original have recently been published[2]—and closely related to one of the most widely read books in the Medieval literature of the Old World, the *Alexander Romance*.[3] Unlike most late Egyptian stories, "The Dream of Nectanebo" deals with an event of recent history, the Persian defeat of Nectanebo II (360–341 B.C.E.) and reconquest of Egypt (late 340s B.C.E.), which marked the end of an independent, native-ruled Egypt.

1. The standard edition of the Greek text is Ludwig Koenen, "The Dream of Nektanebos," *Bulletin of the American Society of Papyrologists* 22 (1985): 171–94.

2. Kim Ryholt, "A Demotic Version of Nectanebo's Dream (P. Carlsberg 562)," *Zeitschrift für Papyrologie und Epigraphik* 122 (1998): 197–200.

3. Beverly Berg, "An Early Source of the *Alexander Romance*," *Greek, Roman, and Byzantine Studies* 14 (1973): 381–87.

[Defense of] Petisis, the hieroglyph carver, to Nectanebo, the king.[4]

Year 17, Pharmouthi 21 or 22, and in the religious calendar, at the full moon.[5]

When Nectanebo, the king, had come to Memphis and sacrificed and asked the gods to reveal to him what had been determined, he dreamt that a boat made of papyrus, which is called in Egyptian "romps," came to anchor at Memphis. There was a large throne on the boat and on the throne sat Isis, the famous benefactress, the discoverer of cultivated crops, and mistress of the gods. And all the gods in Egypt stood beside her, on the right and left of her.

One of the gods came into the center. He seemed to be twenty-one cubits in height and was called in Egyptian Onouris,[6] and in Greek Ares. He prostrated himself and spoke as follows: "Come to me, O Isis, goddess of gods, who possesses the greatest power and rules the world and preserves all the gods and is full of joy, and hear me. As you ordered, I have preserved the land without failing. And even until now I have continued to take every precaution, but Nectanebo, who was made king at the same time by you, has neglected my temple and resisted my decrees. I stay outside my own temple and the contents of the sanctuary, which is called Phersos, are neglected because of the negligence of the person in charge of it." The mistress of the gods, after hearing what had been reported, made no answer.

Nectanebo awakened suddenly in the midst of his dream and urgently ordered that a message be sent to the high priest and the prophet of Onouris at Sebennytos, which is in the interior of the country. When they were present in his audience chamber, the king asked what works still remained in the sanctuary, which is called Phersos. When they said that: "Everything is finished except the carving of the hieroglyphic inscriptions on the stone works," he ordered that they urgently write to the hieroglyph carvers in the famous temples in Egypt. When they had come into his presence as

---

4. For the proper interpretation of the title see Koenen, 191–92.
5. July 5/6, 343 B.C.E.
6. Warrior god from This near Abydos.

they had been instructed, the king inquired who among them was the most skilled and able to complete quickly the work remaining in the sanctuary, which is called Phersos.

One of them from the city of Aphrodite in the Aphroditopolite nome, whose name was Petisis and whose father was Ergeus, said that, if he was appointed, he would be able to complete the work in a few days. The king similarly inquired also of the other craftsmen, and they all said that [the man] spoke the truth and that there was not to be found in the land one like this one.

After the king had assigned the previously indicated tasks to him, [he gave] him a large fee and at the same time encouraged him in order that he accomplish the work in a few days just as he said he would do because of the desire of the god.

Petisis took with him many wine jars and came to Sebennytos. And he thought, because he was by nature a lover of drink, that he should relax before he entered on his task. And it happened that while he was walking about near the south wall of the temple that he observed Athyrepse, the daughter of [. . .], who was the most beautiful in appearance of [the beautiful women] in that [place].

Unfortunately, Apollonius was a devotee of dream interpretation, so he failed to copy the rest of the story. The lost conclusion, however, has been convincingly reconstructed.[7] Distracted by Athyrepse, Petisis failed to complete inscribing the temple of Ares/Onuris, thereby causing the Persian victory foretold in the king's dream. As the heading indicates, Petisis explained his failure and its consequences in a speech to Nectanebo, revealing to the king the inevitability of the Persian defeat but predicting also Nectanebo's escape and his future return in the form of a young king who would free Egypt from Persian oppression, as, indeed, happened a decade later when Alexander the Great drove the Persians from Egypt.

---

7. Koenen, 192–93.

CHRISTIAN EGYPT

Two Coptic Stories

There follow two stories, translated from the Coptic, giving episodes in the life of Pisentius, bishop of Coptos and one of the principal figures in Coptic literary and cultural history.

Born in 568 C.E., the son of a farmer, Pisentius became a monk early in life, having become noted even in childhood for his piety and austerity; thereafter he lived as a solitary in caves or tombs, and then joined a religious community at Tsenti, about twenty miles north of Thebes. It was in these years that his great reputation for holiness and asceticism was established. In about 598 C.E. he was made bishop of the diocese of Coptos, an ancient and important city some thirty miles north of Thebes. Pisentius was famous as a miracle worker who could exorcise demons and heal the sick. More prosaically, as bishop he was reputed to be an effective preacher and administrator, who displayed particular concern for the poor of his diocese. During the period of Sassanid Persian rule in Egypt (619–29 C.E.), he took refuge with a single attendant, John the Elder, in the monastery at Jeme near Thebes (see p. 106, note 1). Although he seems not to have returned to his diocese, his numerous surviving letters reveal that Pisentius continued to deal with the problems of his diocese from his place of exile at Jeme. He died about 632 C.E., and was buried beside the monastery of Tsenti.

Biographies of Pisentius were written by his disciple, John the Elder, and Bishop Moses, his successor to the see of Coptos, and versions of these works survive in both Coptic and Arabic. Like other lives of holy Copts, the biographies of Pisentius consist chiefly of miracles wrought by or through the bishop.

In translating I have not hesitated to restore the sense from the Arabic versions here and there where the Coptic texts are faulty.

Saint Pisentius and the Jealous Man

It happened one day that the spirit of jealousy alighted upon the heart of a man, and he became jealous about his wife: the Devil, hater of the good, who longs to do evil to the nature of mankind, cast scandal into the heart of her husband against a certain man as though he had had intercourse with her. But the woman was innocent of that sin, and the man also was innocent of the impurity which had been imputed to him with regard to the woman, even as the story will inform us if we go forward.

The man cast his wife out because of the evil which he imagined against her. His father and mother made every effort without being able to persuade the man to live with her, even as the wise man Solomon says, "The heart of her husband was full of jealousy."[1]

Not to prolong the story unduly, the matter then reached the

---

1. Compare Prov. 6:34 (Sa'idic-Coptic version).

ears of the clergy of his village, and they excluded him from taking part in the Holy Mysteries.[2] The clergy informed my holy Father about the matter; and my Father sent for him, saying, "Bestir yourself and come to me, and I will find you the necessary answer [to your suspicions]." The man cried out in the village, walking from place to place, breaking out into a rage and saying, "I will not go to Pisentius; what has Pisentius to do with me?" for that man was an inhabitant of Coptos.

And when he persisted in uttering cries angrily until the sun went to its setting on that day, then God, who said by the prophet, "Cast judgment upon me; I will repay, saith the Lord,"[3] brought a fearful disorder on that man in the night. It tormented his entrails, and suffering agony and crying out in a loud voice he said, "Take me to my Father Pisentius; I tell you that it is because of him that this has befallen me. Father, please help me, for I have come down to the straits of death, and if you do not take me to him I shall find no relief." His father and mother despaired of him, thinking that he would die. They said, "Let us prevail upon him [the saint], even if he [our son] lives, since he had said, 'Take me to Father Pisentius the bishop.' At all events if we take him to him he will make the sign of the cross over him and he will stop being tormented." Now it was the beginning of the time that my Father was bishop.

And they brought him up to the monastery to my Father, and they knocked at the door. I went out to them, and his father said to me, "John, if you have ever had regard for me please inform the great man, otherwise my son runs the risk of death, and I believe by God that if he makes the sign of the cross over my son he will find relief straightway. And he has begged me, saying, 'Take me to Father Pisentius the bishop, and I shall be healed, for it is because of him that I am tormented. If I have uttered a word against him in my stupidity, it is because I am ignorant.'"

His son also cried out to me, saying, "O John, please announce me to the great man, for the straits of death have come upon me.

---

2. The Eucharist.
3. Rom. 12:19.

Behold, you see me in my sore need. Why was my mouth not closed, and why did I not die before I uttered a word on that day? Go quickly and inform my lord Father Pisentius of my suffering. Help me, do not leave me to die at your door."

When I heard these things from the man and his son I went in and informed my Father about the man and his son. He said to me, "Leave him alone until he frames his request properly, for he is an ignorant man." I answered him, "If we leave him any longer he will die, for little breath is left in him, and as I see it he has framed his request."

My Father said to me, "Let him come in," and when he and his father had come in he cast himself down at my Father's feet for a long time. My Father said to him, "Rise up, ignorant one." The man answered, "As the Lord lives, if I spend yet three days prostrate at your feet, unless you set your foot upon my head I will not rise up." My Father seized the hair of his head and stood him up, and said to him, "Rise up. See, the Lord will bestow healing upon you if you still obey me." The man answered, "By the straits from which your prayers have saved me, if I have another year or two of life I will never dare to disobey you."

My Father said, "It is because you cast your wife out for nothing that these things have come upon you; of the matter which you have imagined against her and the man both of these are innocent. But I tell you that if you wish to be convinced in your mind about her, and the man about whom you have imagined evil in connection with her—since, my son, man regards the face only, while God regards the heart—when you go home take your wife back into your house; God will make it easy for you and her. And I think that she is pregnant and will bear you a son, and the thing that has been said about her is not true, but, believe me, she is free of guilt. But if she should bear a girl do not stay with her, but cast her out, for then she is not innocent of the sin which has been imputed to her, but has violated her wedlock. But if it is a male child that she bears the thing that has been imputed to her is not true, and she is innocent of what has been imagined against her. But if you wish to bind her by an oath I do not forbid you, for thus does the law of God command: 'If a man's wife transgresses and he is ignorant of it, and a man sleeps with her carnally and it is concealed from her husband and he does not know it, and she has not become pregnant and no witness rises up against her, then she shall be taken to the priest, and he shall bind her by the oath, and he shall give her the water of the curse, and she shall drink it. If the thing that has been cast against her is true, that water will make the skin of her body peel off in leprosy; but if she has been slandered she will be pregnant with a boy.'[4] Now, therefore, my son, if you are not convinced make her swear; I do not forbid you."

The man answered, saying, "From the moment that your Paternity spoke to me my heart was already convinced, and I shall never again cease to obey you."

And he saluted and came away from him and went home with his father, giving glory to God and the saint, Father Pisentius, and when he got home he made peace with his wife. And she brought forth a son, according to the word of the apostolic Father Pisentius. And the man called the name of his son Pisentius, and he remained with his wife from that day to the day of his death.

And the saint had performed three miracles, one better than the other, namely: he saved the woman from the false slander which had been imagined against her; and he freed the man [the alleged adulterer] from guilt; and he cleansed the heart of her husband from the guile of Satan, and so caused those who were in wedlock to be at peace with one another again.

---

4. Compare Num. 5:12–28.

Saint Pisentius and the Mummy

It happened one day, while my Father and I were still in the monastery of Jeme,[1] that my Father said to me, "John, my son, arise, follow me that I may show you the place in which I will dwell in solitude, so that you may visit me every Saturday and bring me a little food, and a little water to drink, for the support of my body." My Father arose and walked in front of me, meditating on the Holy Scriptures, the inspirations of God.

When we had walked about three miles, as I estimated it, we came upon a place which was like a wide-open door. When we had passed into that place we found it like carved stone, with six pillars supporting the rock, it being 52 cubits [about 90 feet] wide, and four-square, and also its height being proportionate, and there

---

1. A town on the west bank of the Nile across from Thebes (modern Luxor); in Pisentius' time this town was a thriving center and important destination for refugees from the Persian invasion. Even after the Muslim conquest of 641, the town remained a Christian center.

being many mummified bodies in it. If you were merely to pass through that place you would smell a quantity of perfumes diffused by the bodies. We took the mummies and piled them one upon another, and then the place was quite clear. The place where the bodies were was like a place that had been highly decorated. The first mummy, which was by the door, the garments in which it was bandaged were of the pure silk of kings, and it was very thick, and its fingers and toes were bandaged separately.

My Father said, "How many years ago did these die, and to which provinces did they belong?" I said to him, "God knows." My Father said to me, "Go away, my son, and dwell in your monastery, take heed for yourself. This world is vanity, and at any time we may be parted from it. Have care for your wretched estate, and prolong your fasting, making it complete, and recite your prayers well, those proper to each time, even as I have taught you, and do not come hither to me except on Saturdays only." And when he had said these things to me I departed.

As I was leaving him I examined one of the pillars, and I found a book, a little scroll of vellum. When my Father had unrolled it he read in it, and found the names of all the people who were buried there written in it; he gave it back to me and I laid it down in its place. I saluted my Father and left him; I walked while he showed me out saying to me, "Be diligent in the work of God, that he may show mercy to your wretched soul. Now do you see these mummies? Everyone must needs become thus. Some there are now in Hades, whose sins were great. Some of these are in the outer darkness, others are in pits and wells full of fire, others are in the lowest Hades, others again are in the river of fire; they have never yet been given any rest. Then again, there are others who are in places of rest, in accordance with their deeds, which were good. When man goes out of this world what is past is past." When he had said these things to me he said, "Pray for me, O my son, until I see you again." Then I came to my dwelling-place, and I stayed, acting according to the commandment of my holy Father Pisentius.

And on the next Saturday I filled the pitcher of water, and [took] a little moistened wheat, according to the measure of food that he had ordered. [For] he had decided upon two ephahs and had divided them up for the forty days [of Lent]; he had taken a measuring-cup and measured [the portions], saying, "When you come on a Saturday bring this amount [of wheat] with the water, and visit me." Then I took the jug of water and the little moistened wheat, and I went into the place where he was dwelling in solitude. When I had drawn near his dwelling-place I heard someone weeping and beseeching my Father in great trouble of mind, saying, "I beseech you, my lord Father, beseech the Lord on my behalf that I may be released from these punishments and that I may not be taken to them again, for I have suffered greatly." I supposed that it was a man who was talking to my Father, for the place was dark; and I sat down and listened to my Father, with whom a mummy was speaking, the one whom I mentioned as being by the door.

My Father said to the mummy, "To which province do you belong?" He said, "I am from the city of Armant."[2] My father said to him, "Who was your father?" He said "My father was Agricolus, and my mother was Eustathia." My Father asked him, "Whom did they worship?" And he said, "They worshipped him who is in the waters, namely Poseidon." My Father said to him, "Did you not hear before you died that Christ had come to the world?" He said "No, my Father, my parents were pagans, and I myself followed their way of life. Woe, woe is me that I was born into the world! Why did not my mother's womb become my grave? But it befell me, when I was come to the straits of death, the first who surrounded me were the World Governors;[3] they told all the evils that I had done, and they said to me, 'Let them come now and deliver you from the punishments to which you will be subjected.' They had iron hooks in their hands, and also pointed iron spikes like spears, and they were stabbing my sides with them, and gnashing their teeth at me.

"After a little my eyes opened and I saw Death hanging in the air in many forms. And forthwith the pitiless angels drew my miserable soul out of my body, and they bound it to the tail of a ghostly

---

2. Ancient Hermonthis, an important administrative center on the West bank of the Nile, south of modern Luxor.

3. An order of spirits.

black horse and dragged me to the west. O, woe is every sinner like me who has been born into the world! O, my lord Father, into the hands of how many pitiless torturers, each one different in form, did they deliver me! O how many wild beasts did I see in the path, O how many tormenting powers! When they had carried me into outer darkness I saw a great place dug more than two hundred cubits deep, full of reptiles, each one of them with seven heads and their whole bodies covered with stings like scorpions. There were also great worms there, very great and terrible to look upon, with fangs in their mouths like iron stakes. I was taken and cast before the worm there which never sleeps, and he devoured me continually, while all the wild beasts were gathered together with him, and when he filled his mouth all the wild beasts who surrounded me filled their mouths too."[4]

My Father said to him, "Since you died until today, have they given you no rest, nor left you for a little without hurting you?"

The mummy said, "Yes, my Father, they have mercy every Saturday and Sunday[5] on all who are under punishment. When Sunday is over they cast us again into punishments suited to us, and we forget the years that we spent in the world. Afterwards, if we are not conscious of the pain of this punishment they subject us to another which is more painful. But when you prayed for me, immediately the Lord commanded those who were scourging me and they plucked from my mouth the iron bit which was put upon me; they released me and I came to you. See, I have told you the conditions in which I have been. O my lord Father, pray for me, that I may be given a little rest, and not be carried off to that place again."

My Father said to him, "The Lord is compassionate and merciful, he will have mercy on you. Return then, and sleep until the day of the general resurrection of everybody, when all men will arise and you yourself will arise with them."

God is witness to these words, O my brothers, that I saw the

---

4. The descriptions of the mummy's punishments in the afterlife may reflect the paintings in the ancient tombs near Thebes, which monks visited, as in the story, or sometimes even inhabited. We owe this suggestion to Professor Terry Wilfong of the University of Michigan.

5. "From the ninth hour of Saturday to the end of Sunday," says the Arabic version.

mummy with my own eyes, and he lay down in his place as formerly. And I, when I had seen these things, I marveled greatly and
gave glory to God. I called out before entering, according to the
rule, saying, "Bless me," and I went in and kissed his hands and
feet. He said to me, "John, how long ago did you come here? Have
you seen anyone, or heard anyone speaking to me?" And I said "No,
my Father." He said to me, "You have uttered a falsehood, like
Gehazi, when he uttered falsehood to the prophet, saying, 'Thy servant has not gone anywhere.'[6] But if you have seen or heard anything, if you tell it to any man in my lifetime you are excommuni-
cated."

I concealed the matter, and I have not dared to tell it until today.

---

6. 2 Kings 5:25.

MUSLIM EGYPT

عمّ متولّى

«عمّ متولّى» ، بائعُ اللّبّ والفول السودانى
والحَلوَى ، بائعٌ متنقّل يعرفه سكانُ «الحلمية» ومايجاورها
من الجهات ، يسير ببضاعته البيضاء الطويلة ، وجلبابه
الواسع الأكمام ، تساوى المَيْنة ، وقد حمل على ظهره
قُفّته الضيقة ، وهو ينادى مُعدّدًا للأطفال أصناف
بضاعته بلهجة السودانيين ، بصوتٍ وانٍ أضعفه الفقر
والهَرَم ، إلا أنه لمّا يزلْ محتفظاً بنبْرة الآمر ؛ فقد
نشأ الرجل فى السودان ، وحارب فى صفوف المهديّين
برتبة قائد فِرقة . وقد عاش طول عمره وحيداً . ليس

Tales of Recompense

THE KITAB AL MUKAFA'A, or Book of Recompense, was written by Abu Ja'far Ahmad ibn Yusuf, known as Ibn ad-Daya, "the Son of the Midwife." He was a scribe in the service of the Tulunid dynasty in Egypt,[1] and the author of several works, including a history of the Tulunids, a book on the *Politics* of Plato, and histories of medical practitioners and astrologers, as well as a number of poems. He died in 951 C.E. The following extracts are taken from his biography as given in the *Dictionary of Learned Men,* compiled by the early thirteenth-century writer, Yaqut al-Hamawi. It consists of quotations from contemporary and near-contemporary sources:

> ". . . His father Yusuf ibn Ibrahim, known as Abu'l-Hasan, was one of the leading scribes in Egypt. . . . He was of perfect manliness and famous loyalty.
> ". . . Abu Ja'far Ahmad ibn Yusuf . . . was one of the most excellent and the most famous of the people of Egypt, a man of wide knowledge in literature, medicine, astrology, arithmetic and other sciences. . . . He was of outstanding versatility, a chief among the eloquent scribes, the arithmeticians and the astrologers, an authority on the *Almagest* and Euclid, pleasant in companionship, skillful in poetry. . . ."

His Book of Recompense is a collection of seventy-one stories, divided into three parts and designed to illustrate the principle that good and bad deeds find their recompense. All the stories are ostensibly true, and Ibn ad-Daya is careful to quote his sources for every tale. Several of the stories are personal experiences of the author and of his immediate family circle. The telling of the stories is exclusively his own. Unlike many Arabic collectors of anecdotes, Ibn ad-Daya is not content merely to reproduce his stories as he received them. He tells them in his own words and in his own way, with a simplicity, a realism and a sensitiveness that mark him apart in an age when floridity, intricacy and artifice were the most admired qualities in prose style. The first printed edition was issued in Cairo in 1914, from a unique manuscript. An annotated edition for schools appeared in 1941.

---

1. The Tulunids were a dynasty of independent governors of Turkish origin, who ruled Egypt from 868 to 905. The first ruler was Ahmad ibn Tulun (868–83), the second Khumarawaih (883–95).

A Merchant and His Wife

This story was told me by Ahmad ibn Ayman, the secretary of Ahmad ibn Tulun:

In Basra once I entered the house of a merchant whose name I forget, and I saw his two sons, in extremity of cleanliness. When he saw me staring at them he said [fearing the evil eye]: "I wish you would invoke the protection of God upon them." I did so, and said to him, "You chose the mother well and your issue is comely." He answered "There is no uglier woman in all Basra than their mother nor any that I love more dearly. There is concerning her and me a strange tale." I asked him to tell it me, and he said:

"I used to live in Ubulla, where I made a scanty living. Then I carried merchandise from there to Basra and I made a profit. Then I carried some back from Basra to Ubulla and again made a profit. So I went on trading between the two till my wealth became considerable and my good fortune became known. I preferred to live in Basra, and I learned that it was not proper for me to dwell there without a wife. Now there was no man of greater position in Basra than the grandfather of these two lads, and he had a daughter whom he kept from marrying, meeting her suitors with hostility. I told myself to approach him concerning her, so I called on him privately and said to him: 'O my uncle, I am Such a one, son of Such a one the merchant!' And he answered: 'Your house and your father's house are not unknown to us.' I said: 'I have come to seek your daughter in marriage.' He answered: 'By God, I have nothing against you, but many of the great ones of Basra have come to me to ask for her, and I refused them. Indeed, I do not wish to send her from my bosom to one who will appraise her as slaves are appraised.' I said: 'May God raise her above such an estate! I ask you to take me among your people and include me among your household.' He asked: 'Must it be so?' and I answered: 'It must, and it would be an added favor that you would confer on me.' He said: 'Come to me tomorrow with your people.'

"I left him and went to a gathering of merchants of consequence, and I asked them to come with me on the morrow. They said: 'You are urging us to wasted effort,' but I insisted that they should come with me. So they came, certain of a rebuff. We went there on the next day, and he greeted us in a most friendly manner and accepted me as bridegroom, slaughtering beasts and feasting the people. Then they went, and he said to me: 'If you wish to pass the night with your wife, do so, for there is nothing that calls for delay.' I answered: 'This, my master, is what I desire.' He went on speaking to me in all friendliness until the hour of the evening prayers. He led me in our orisons, then he praised God and I did likewise; he prayed and I prayed, until the time of the night prayer came, and again he led me in prayer. Then he took me by the hand and led me into a most sumptuously appointed house with servants and slave-girls, all exceedingly clean. No sooner had I sat down than he rose and said: 'I entrust you to God, and may God grant you both well-being and all success.' Then some old women of his household gathered round me and displayed his daughter to me, and what I saw was of no great excellence. Then they drew the curtains about us, and she said: 'O my master, I am one of my father's secrets which he hid from other men. Then he revealed it to you, esteeming you a fit person to guard it. Do not discredit his opinion in this. If that which is sought in a wife is beauty of form rather than beauty of conduct and chastity, then great is my ordeal, for it is my hope that I have more of the latter than I lack of the former.' Then she rose and brought a bag of money and said: 'O my master, God has permitted you three wives beside myself and as many concubines as you desire. You will be able to marry the wives and buy the slave-girls with the money in this bag. I dedicate it to your passions, and I ask nothing of you save that you do not divorce me.'"

Ahmad said: The merchant swore to me:

"She obtained a dominion over my heart such as no comely one could win by her comeliness. I said to her: 'You shall hear from me now the reward for what you have offered. By God, I shall never take any woman other than you. I shall make you my portion in this world in those things which a man requires of a woman.' She was the tenderest, most trustworthy and best-conducted of women in all that she did in my house. I saw clearly that it was better so, as the years came upon me and my need of what is right grew greater than my need of lovemaking. God has rewarded me for my response to her noble words and deeds, and has given me by her these two fine sons. We revere Him for His bounty and His generosity towards us."

One of the Kings of India
and a Merchant

I was told this tale by Mansur ibn Isma'il, the jurist in the Sacred Law:

A man whom we know set out with merchandise for India, and he returned to us in the extremity of joy with costly perfumes of many kinds. We asked him: "What profit did you make on the merchandise with which you set forth?" He answered: "I and all those who were with me were shipwrecked and, when I despaired of my life, I was cast upon one of the islands of India. There I was met by a crowd of people, who took me before their king. He said to me: 'You have lost the gift that was external to you. Now what have you that is of your very self?' I replied: 'I have writing and arithmetic.' The king said: 'What you have kept is better than what you have lost. It would be well for you to teach my son Arabic writing and arithmetic, and it is my desire to give you in compensation more than you have lost.' Then he entrusted to me his most intelligent and agreeable son, and the lad learned in a short time what others learn in a long time.

"Now when the king saw that he made progress and that I had earned his gratitude, he sent his friend to me, saying: 'I have a gift for you from the king.' Then he brought in a heifer and said: 'Let me give it to the herdsman for you.' I said: 'Do so,' and in my eyes the king's deed was small beside the greatness of his state. Not long had passed before the herdsman came to me and said: 'The cow is dead,' and all the king's courtiers greeted me with regret and commiseration. Then his son made further progress and he sent me another heifer which again I gave to the herdsman. A short time passed and he came to me with good tidings, saying: 'The cow is in calf.' When her bearing was done she calved and the court assembled and congratulated me. Then the king sat in public audience and sent for all the merchandise which you see with me, and said:

"'I am not unaware of what is due to you for the education of my son, nor did I send the first cow because of the virtue of cows in my estimation; but ill luck befell you at sea and robbed you of all your property. Therefore I tested your fortune with the heifer, for I knew that if I were to give you all that I possess and your ill luck remained, it would all perish and be lost to you. When I heard that she had died I knew that you were still accursed. Then I tested your fortune with the second heifer, and when I learned that she was in calf I knew that the ill fortune was leaving you. Then I rejoiced for you and awaited her calving. When she dropped a normal, sound-limbed calf I knew that you were delivered from your ill fortune. This is what I have prepared for you.' And so he presented me with perfumes which I assessed at twenty thousand dinars and put me to sea. I had a safe journey, and the price of the goods increased in the land of the Arabs above the figure I mentioned."

Mansur said: "When I saw him he had achieved affluence and an ample livelihood."

The Midwife of Khumarawaih and Her Sister

Umm Asya, the midwife of the children of Khumarawaih ibn Tulun (a woman of religion and piety and in favor with Khumarawaih) told me this tale, when we were speaking of the goodness of Almighty God in giving His servants sustenance and protection:

Two brothers married my sister and myself. My sister's husband was favored by fortune, mine was not. He died in poor circumstances, leaving me daughters only and barely enough money to arrange the funeral. My sister's husband died, but he left money, houses and vessels to his children.

I toiled to provide for my children, but sometimes when my affairs went badly I went to my sister and said: "Lend me so much and so much"—for I was ashamed to say to her: "Give me." Then the month of Ramadan came, and when it was half gone my daughters besought me to give them sweetmeats for the festival. So I went to my sister and said to her: "Lend me a dinar to make sweetmeats for my children," and she answered: "O my sister, you anger me with your 'lend me'; if I lend it to you, where will you find the money to pay me back? From the revenues of your houses or the produce of your garden? It would be better if you said 'give me.'" I said to her: "I shall repay you by the grace of Almighty God, which cannot be reckoned, and His bounty which is given when least expected." Then she mocked me, saying: "By God, these are wishes, my sister, and wishes are the merchandise of fools." So I left, dragging my feet wearily, and returned to my house.

Now, there was in our neighborhood a negro servant of Bint al-Yatim, the wife of Khumarawaih. No sooner had I reached our street than he said to me: "There is in our quarter a woman in labor whose cries have grieved my heart. Go to her, for she has no midwife." By God, I had never before tended a woman in labor, but I went in and stroked her belly and made her sit as the midwives had made me sit when I was in labor. So she gave birth in due time, and when her cries ceased the servant came and asked concerning her, and I said: "She has given birth." He was astonished at the speed of her affair and thought that this was something I had achieved by skillful treatment and wise handling. Then he went to his mistress, Bint al-Yatim, who was then big with the first-born of Khumarawaih. Midwives had been brought to her and had displeased her. He said to her: "There is a midwife in our neighborhood whom we brought to a woman in labor in our street. She placed her hand on her belly, and her child was born." And so he described me, ascribing to me powers which are beyond any save only Almighty God. She answered the servant: "Bring her to me tomorrow." So the servant came to me and summoned me to his mistress. I accepted joyfully, trusting in God. My soul was lightened and said: "The decree of Blessed and Almighty God is in this to the end." Later she complained of the pains which are suffered by women in childbirth. I put my hands inside her garments and stroked her belly while secretly beseeching God to grant me success. Those of her people who heard my prayers thought I was weaving spells. Her pain was eased and she was greatly pleased. Then Khumarawaih came in to see her and said: "What ailed you?" And she answered: "A colic in my belly, but a midwife whom I sent for placed her hand on it and my pain ceased." So she presented me to him (he was near to his wife), and he said to me: "I hope that Almighty God will save her by your blessing."

We entered upon the last ten days of Ramadan, and I entrusted myself to God even more than does the traveler in the mountains, for fear lest my sister rejoice in my discomfiture. When no more than three days had passed, her pains began and I placed her on the chair of childbirth. Her labor lasted but two hours and was easy, and she bore a son. Meanwhile, Khumarawaih was rising and sitting, going and coming. When she gave birth she expected fearful pain in her bearing, and when it happened she said to me: "Is this childbirth?" And I answered her: "Yes." Then God knows, she kissed my eyes in her joy. Meanwhile, Khumarawaih cried out: "O blessed woman, give me news of her," and I said: "By the prince's life, she is in good health, and by the grace of God she has borne a sound, sturdy boy." Then he gave me a thousand dinars and in his excess of solicitude insisted on seeing her. I made him wait till I removed the appurtenances of childbirth, and I said to her: "My lady, smile to him when you see him." And when he came in she smiled to him. He gave much money in alms for her and for his son.

When the seventh day came (it fell one day before the festival) she ordered five hundred dinars to be given to me, and I received another thousand from her followers, two thousand five hundred dinars in all. More than thirty robes of honor were conferred upon me and upon the rest of her household, and three special trays of food prepared for the festival were brought to me. Then I departed to my house and I sent a tray to my sister. She came to congratulate me, containing her pride. I showed her the money and fine robes and delicacies which I had earned, and I said to her: "My sister, you reproached me for saying 'lend me'; it is from these gifts that I would repay you. Do not belittle those who rely on God for sustenance and place their trust and hopes in Him."

This woman earned much money through her post with Khumarawaih, and fulfilled important duties for a number of the great ones of the city.

The *Abridgement of Marvels* is an Arabic work of uncertain authorship and date, sometimes attributed to the historian Mas'udi (d. 956). It was almost certainly written in Egypt, probably not later than the eleventh century, and contains a medley of fact and legend, in which the latter element predominates, concerning the marvels of geography and history. The Arabic text is still in manuscript, but an almost idential text was published in Cairo in 1357/1938 under the title *Akhbar al-Zaman*. More than half of the book is devoted to the *Wonders of Egypt,* a largely mythical account of the history of Egypt before the coming of the Arabs. The real history of ancient Egypt seems by this time to have been entirely forgotten, and the author of the abridgement is content with a series of miracles and myths culled, it would appear, from Coptic traditions and writings. This legendary history, with its strange events and supernatural happenings, is repeated with variations by almost all the historians of Muslim Egypt, and it was not until the nineteenth century that a study of European works of scholarship restored to the Egyptians the lost chapters of their own record.

Another work of the same kind is the *Egyptian History* of Murtada ibn al-Khafif. A French translation, from an Arabic manuscript in the library of Cardinal Mazarin, was published in 1666 by Pierre Vattier, "Docteur en Médecine, Lecteur et Professeur du Roi en Langue Arabique." An English version from the French was produced in 1672 by J. Davies of Kidwelly under the title: THE EGYPTIAN HISTORY, Treating of the PYRAMIDS, the Inundation of the *Nile* and other PRODIGIES of EGYPT, According to the *Opinions* and *Traditions* of the ARABIANS, Written Originally in the *Arabian* Tongue by *Murtadi* the Son of *Gaphiphus*.

Little is known about the author of the book, though from internal evidence he would appear to have been a thirteenth-century Egyptian. By a strange chance, the Arabic text on which Vattier based his translation has disappeared, and since no other manuscript is known the work has survived only in the French and English versions.

The following extracts from the *Abridgement of Marvels* are translated from a manuscript of the Arabic text in the Bodleian Library, Oxford. The passages from the *Egyptian History* are in the version of J. Davies.

The Image that Exposed Adulterers
(From the *Abridgement of Marvels*)

KING MANQA'US made an image of a magical bird with out-spread wings, in gilded copper, and placed it on a column in the center of the town. No adulterer or adulteress could pass by it without revealing his shame. The people were thus tested by it, and refrained from adultery for fear of it. They continued so until the time of King Kalkan,[1] who lost and destroyed its power.

This was how it happened. There was a woman among his wives who sinned against him, lusting for a man of the king's servants. She feared lest the king should hear of this and put her to the test of the statue, whereby she would be disgraced and put to death. She cast about her for some ruse to avert this. One night when the king was with her and they were drinking together, she began to speak of wanton women, blaming and reviling them. The king

---

1. The reading of this name is doubtful.

spoke of this statue, of its usefulness to the people, and of the praise and gratitude which were due to it. She said: "It is so, and the king has spoken truly, yet Manqa'us did not act rightly in this." "How so?" he asked, and she replied: "In this respect, that he wearied himself and his sages in accomplishing something for the good of the vulgar, without thinking of his own advantage. This was the weakness of old age. The wise course would have been to erect the image in the abode of the king, amid his wives and slave-girls; then if one of them were guilty of a crime, the king would have known of it and would have punished her secretly, without anything becoming known to the vulgar, and it would have been a deterrent to whoever in his palace was overcome by her passions, perhaps only once in her lifetime. For the passions of women are stronger and more frequent than those of men, since their intelligence is weaker. Now, on the other hand, if such a thing should happen in the king's palace (the Higher Light forfend), the test would shame the king himself and make the affair known to the great and the vulgar alike. If he punished without testing, he would transgress, and if he suffered it, he would suffer a sin."

The king said: "You have spoken truly in what you have said." He regarded her words as good counsel and true speaking, believing that she was hinting at something of which she knew, but which she did not wish to reveal directly. The next day he removed the statue from its place and erected it in his palace, in a place which he assigned to it without deliberation and without consulting any sage or learned man. When it was erected in the palace he made several tests, and nothing resulted from them. Then the king repented of having moved it, while his slave-girl was able to abandon herself without fear to the evil passions that raged within her.

Such works of magic must only be carried out after observing the stars, choosing their right positions and ascertaining the correct time for such things.

A Visit to the Source of the Nile

THERE WAS A MAN of the house of Esau, called Ha'id, son of Abu Salum, son of Esau, son of Isaac, son of Abraham—upon him be peace—who fled before a certain king and came to the land of Egypt. He stayed there for some years, and when he saw the wonders of the Nile and the benefits it brings he swore before Almighty God that he would follow its bank until he reached its source or die on the way.

He walked along the bank—some say for thirty years without diverging from his course, and some say for fifteen years this way and fifteen years that way—until he reached a lake and saw the Nile before him. He went up to the shore of the lake, and met a man standing and praying under an apple-tree. He greeted him courteously, and the man by the tree asked him: "Who are you?" to which he replied: "I am Ha'id son of Abu Salum son of Esau son of Isaac son of Abraham—upon him be peace. And who are you—may God be good to you?" He said: "I am 'Imran. What has brought you to this distant place, O Ha'id? God revealed to me that I should stay in this place until I die." Ha'id said: "Tell me, 'Imran, what do you know of this Nile? Have you heard tell of any of the sons of Adam who reached its source?" 'Imran replied: "It is said that a man sprung from Esau will reach it, and I think that this can be none other than you, Ha'id." "Show me the way, 'Imran," said Ha'id, and 'Imran answered: "I shall not tell you unless you grant me what I ask of you." "What is that, 'Imran?" he asked, and 'Imran replied: "If you return to me and find me still living, stay with me until God reveals something to me concerning you. If God causes me to die, bury me." "I promise you that," said Ha'id, and 'Imran continued: "Go straight on beside this lake, and you will reach a place where there is a Beast of which you will see the beginning, but not the end. Be not affrighted, but mount it. It is a Beast that is an enemy of the Sun, and pounces upon it to swallow it when it rises and when it sets, but is held back by the heat. When you have mounted this Beast, ride it until you reach the Nile again. Then dismount, and you will find a land of iron, with mountains, trees and plains of iron. You will cross it, and come upon a land of copper, with mountains, trees and plains of copper. You will cross that, and come upon a land of silver, with mountains, trees and plains of silver. When you have crossed that, you will reach a land of gold, with mountains, trees and plains of gold, and it is there that you will attain the Knowledge of the Nile." Ha'id journeyed until he reached the land of iron, then the land of copper, then the land of silver, then the land of gold, and he walked therein until he reached a golden wall with golden battlements and a golden dome, and with four gates. He saw water falling from this wall and gathering under the dome, where it divided and flowed away in four rivers. Three of them disappeared into the earth and one burst along the surface of the earth. It was the Nile. He drank of its waters and rested. Then he leapt at the wall and sought to reach the other side, but an angel appeared and said: "No further, O Ha'id! You have attained the Knowledge of this Nile, and this place is Paradise." Ha'id said: "I would like to look upon what is in Paradise." The angel answered: "You cannot go in this day, O Ha'id." He asked: "What is it I see yonder?" The angel answered: "It is the sphere where the sun and the moon revolve. It is in the form of a quern." "I wish to mount it and turn with it," said Ha'id. (Some say that he mounted it while yet in this life, and others say he did not.) The angel said: "O Ha'id, your food will be brought to you from Paradise. Never prefer anything that is of the world before it, for it is not fitting that anything that is of the world should be preferred to that which is of Paradise. It will last you as long as you live." While he was speaking a cluster of grapes descended, of three colors, the color of the green emerald, of the white pearl and of the red hyacinth. The angel continued: "O Ha'id, you have attained the Knowledge of this Nile." Ha'id asked: "What are these three rivers that plunge into the earth?" The angel answered: "One of them is the Euphrates, the second is Saihun, the third is Jaihun."[1]

Ha'id returned and walked until he reached the Beast. He mounted it, and when it pounced upon the setting sun it brought him back to the place where he had first mounted it. He walked again until he reached 'Imran, and found that he had died. He stayed by his grave for three days, and met an aged being in human form, prostrate and weeping by 'Imran. The old man turned to Ha'id and greeted him and said: "O Ha'id, what have you learned of the Knowledge of the Nile?" Ha'id told him, and the man said: "Thus do we find it in the Books." Wondrous apples had appeared on that tree and the old man tempted Ha'id, saying: "Will you not eat of this fruit?" He answered: "I have been given my food from Paradise, and I have been commanded never to prefer anything that is of this world before it." He said: "You speak truth, Ha'id. It is not fitting that anything that is of this world should be preferred to that which is of Paradise. But have you seen such apples as these in this world? God brought this tree from Paradise for 'Imran for his sustenance, and planted it in this earth. It is not of this world, and God left it here for you alone. If you depart, it will be taken away." The old man continued in this wise until Ha'id took an apple and bit it, whereupon

---

1. 1. Cf. Gen. 2:8–14. Saihun and Jaihun in Arabic usually mean the Oxus and Jaxartes.

the angel appeared beside him and said: "Now do you know him who caused your father to leave Paradise? Had you been able to keep these grapes which are with you, the people of the world would have eaten of them and they would not have been consumed. Now you will strive to attain them, as your forefathers strove to attain them."

Ha'id continued his journey until he reached Egypt, and told the people this story. He died. May God have mercy on him.

That is the end of the story, which I have confirmed. There is nothing in it worthy of blame.

Miraculous Stories of the Pyramids

(From the *Egyptian History*)

AFTER THE PYRAMID was open'd people went in out of curiosity for some years, many entering into it, and some returning thence without any inconvenience, others perishing in it. One day it happened that a company of Young men (above 20 in number) swore that they would go into it, provided nothing hindered them, and to force their way to the end of it. They therefore took along with them meat and drink for two moneths: they also took Plates of Iron and Bars, Wax-candles and Lanterns, Match and Oyl, Hatchets, Hooks and other sharp Instruments, and enter'd into the Pyramid: most of them got down from the first Descent and the second, and pass'd along the ground of the Pyramid, where they saw Bats as big as black Eagles, which began to beat their Faces with much violence. But they generously endur'd that inconvenience, and advanc'd still till they came to a Narrow passage, through which came an impetuous wind, and extraordinary cold; yet so as they could not perceive whence it came, nor whither it went. They advanc'd to get into the Narrow place, and then their Candles began to go out, which obliged them to put them into their Lanterns. Then they entered, but the place seemed to be joyn'd and close before them: whereupon one of them said to the rest, "Tie me by the waist with a cord, and I will venture to advance, conditionally that if any accident happen to me, you immediately draw me back." At the entrance of the Narrow place there were great empty vessels made like Coffins, with their lids by them; whence they inferr'd, that those who set them there had prepar'd them for their death; and that to get to their Treasures and Wealth there was a necessity of passing through that Narrow place. They bound their Companion with cords, that he might venture to get through that passage; but immediately the passage clos'd upon him, and they heard the noise of the crushing of his bones: they drew the cords to them, but they could not get him back. Then there came to them a dreadful voice out of that Cave, which startled and blinded them so that they fell down, having neither motion nor sense. They came to themselves awhile after, and endeavoured to get out, being much at a loss what to do. At last after much trouble they returned, save only some of them who fell under the Descent. Being come out into the Plain they sate down together, all astonished at what they had seen, and reflecting on what had happened to them; whereupon the Earth cleft before them, and cast up their dead Companion, who was at first immovable, but two hours after began to move, and spoke to them in a Language they understood not, for it was not the *Arabian*. But some time after one of the Inhabitants of the Upper *Egypt* interpreted it to them, and told them his meaning was this; *This is the reward of those who endeavour to seise what belongs to another.* After these words their Companion seemed dead as before, whereupon they buried him in that place. Some of them died also in the Pyramid. Since that, he who commanded in those parts, having heard of their adventure, they were brought to him, and they related all this to him, which he much wondered at.

Another History relates, that some entered into the Pyramid, and came to the lowest part of it, where they turned round about. There appeared to them a Hollow place, wherein there was a beaten path, in which they began to go. And then they found a Basin, out of which distill'd fresh water, which fell into several Pits which were under the Basin, so as they knew not whence it came, nor whither it went. After that they found a square Hall, the walls whereof were of strange stones of several colours. One of the company took a little stone and put into his mouth, and immediately his ears were deafened. Afterwards they came to a place made like a Cistern full of coined Gold, like a large sort of Cakes that are made; for every piece was of the weight of 1000 Drams. They took some of them, but could not get out of the place till they had returned them into the place whence they had taken them. They afterwards found another place with a great Bench, such as is ordinarily before houses for people to sit on; and on the Bench a Figure of green stone, representing a tall ancient Man sitting, having a large Garment about him, and little Statues before him, as if they were Children whom he taught: they took some of those Figures, but could not get out of the place till they had left them behind them. They passed on along the same way, and heard a dreadful noise and great hurly-burly, which they durst not approach. Then having advanced further, they found a square place, as if it were for some great Assembly, where there were many Statues, and among others the Figure of a Cock made of red Gold: that Figure was dreadful, enameled with Jacinths, whereof there were two great ones in both eyes, which shined like two great Torches: they went near it, and immediately it crew terribly, and began to beat its two wings, and thereupon they heard several voices which came to them on all sides. They kept on their way, and found afterwards an Idol of white stone, with the Figure of a Woman standing on her head, and two lions of white stone lying on each side of her, which seem'd to roar and endeavour to bite. They recommended themselves to God and went on, and kept on their way till they saw a Light; after which going out at an open place, they perceived they were in a great Sandy Desert. At the passage out of that open place there were two Statues of black stone, having Half Pikes in their hands. They were extremely astonish'd, whereupon they began to return towards the East, till they came near the Pyramids on the outside. This happen'd in the time of *Jezid*, the Son of *Gabdolmelic*, the son of *Gabdal*, Governour of *Egypt*,[1] who having heard of it sent some persons with those before spoken of to observe the open place of the Pyramid. They sought it several days, but could never find it again, whereupon they were accounted fools. But they show'd him the head of a Ring, which one of them had taken in the Assembly-place, which they had found in the Pyramid; which obliged him to believe what they said. That head was valued at a great summe of money.

It is further related, that other persons in the time of the Commander *Achemed,* the Son of *Toulon* (God show him mercy) entered in like manner into the Pyramid, and found there a Cruse of red Glass, which they brought away. As they came out they lost one of their Men, which oblig'd them to go in again to look for him. They found him stark naked laughing continually, and saying to them, Trouble not your selves to look for me. After which he got away from them, and return'd into the Pyramid. Whence they inferr'd that the Spirits had distracted him, whereupon they went out and left him there. Upon which they were accused before the Judge, who condemned them to exemplary punishment, and took away from them the Cruse, which had in it four pound of glass. A certain person said thereupon, that the Cruse had not been set in that place for nothing. Which occasioned the filling of it with water, and then being weighed again, it weighed as much as when it was empty, and no more. They afterwards took off some of that water several times, but the Vessel came still to the same weight. Whence they conjectured that it was one of the Wine-vessels whereof the Ancients had made use, and had been made to that purpose by their Sages, and placed there. For the use of Wine was permitted among them. This was a strange miracle.

They relate further several Stories of this kind, and among others that some entered into the Pyramid with a Child to abuse it; and

---

1. Probably a confusion between the Umayyad Caliph Yazid II ibn ʿAbd al-Malik (720–24) and his brother ʿAbdallah ibn ʿAbd al-Malik, governor of Egypt 705–9.

that having committed that sin, there came out against them a black young Man, with a Cudgel in his hand, who beat them furiously, so that they fled leaving there their Meat and their Cloaths. The same thing happen'd to others in the Pyramid of *Achemima.* There entered also into the Pyramid of *Achemima* a Man and a Woman to commit adultery therein; but they were immediately cast along on the ground, and dyed in a Phrensie.

Of Queen Charoba of Egypt and Gebirus the Metapheguian

Gebirus the *Metapheguian* . . . traveled so long till he got near the land of *Egypt*, and approached it at that part where the Queen was willing he should, for he did not contradict her in any thing, his design being to get her to marry him, and by that means to make him King of *Egypt*: or (if she denied him) to dam up with stones the course of the *Nile*, and turn it into another Countrey, and so make the *Egyptians* die of hunger and thirst. *Charoba* sent to him a Servant-maid she had, one who managed her affairs, a very subtile Wench, a great Enchantress, and a Cheat: she saw with him huge Bodies, which there was no means to overcome by fighting; wherefore she advised her Mistress not to engage into a war against him: "I shall endeavor rather (said she) to defeat him by some stratagem, and to carry the business so as he may neither hurt you nor your Subjects." After that she took along with her what was most pleasant in *Egypt*, Conserves, rich Garments, sweet Scents, Arms, Gold and Silver; and with all this desired permission to visit *Gebirus*, which was soon granted her. She presented to him all these Rarities, which he willingly received: Then she told him that the Queen of *Egypt* was in Love with him, and desirous to Marry him, and far from refusing so advantageous a Match. This news made him jocund, and put him into a good humour. He return'd her this answer: "Promise the Queen from me for a Marriage-gift what you please yourself." "The Queen (reply'd she) needs not anything of yours, since your affairs will henceforth be common; but she desires of you instead of a Marriage present, that you cause a City to be built in her Land, on the side of the *Roman* Sea, that it may be an honorable mark to her to the end of the World, and that it may be a discovery of your power; and that you employ in the Building of it these Stones and these Pillars which you have brought with you to dam up the Chanel of the Nile." He granted her Request, and entered into the Land of *Egypt* with his Forces, and founded the City on the West-side, at the place where now *Alexandria* is; to that end encamping himself and his Army on the *Roman* Sea-side. *Charoba* sent him several sorts of Presents and Refreshments. *Alexandria* was then ruin'd, ever since the *Gadites* went out of *Egypt*: for it had been founded by *Sedad*, the son of *Gad*, who had a design to bring thither whatever was most precious in all the quarters of the Earth, for he was the Monarch of the World East and West. But the Destroyer of Castles prevented him, I mean Death, which none can divert or avoid; yet were there some tracks of it as some affirm. *Gebirus* caused to be brought thither the Stones, and the Pillars, and assembled the Artists and the Engineers.

Charoba sent him also a thousand Handy-craftsmen. He spent a long time in Building, so that his money was exhausted, and his people could do no more. For when they had built and made some advancement, as soon as the evening was come, while they took their rest in the night, they were astonish'd in the morning, that they could find no sign of what they had done. For there came out of the Sea certain people who took away all into the salt waters. *Gebirus* was extremely troubled and afflicted thereat. *Charoba* sent him a thousand Goats or Sheep, which were milk'd for the Kings Kitchen. They were kept by a Shepherd belonging to *Gebirus*, of whom he had received that charge. This Shepherd led them out to graze, accompany'd by a great many other Shepherds, upon the Sea side. One day this Shepherd (having put the Beasts into the custody of the other Shepherds, who obeyed him) being a beautiful person, and of a good Aspect and Stature, saw a fair young Lady issuing out of the Sea, which came towards him, and being come very near him saluted him; he return'd the salutation, and she began to speak to him with all imaginable courtesie and civility, and said to him; "Young man, would you wrestle with me for something which I should lay against you?" "What would you lay?" reply'd the Shepherd. "If you give me a fall (says the young Lady) I will be yours, and you shall dispose of me as you please; and if I give you a fall, I will have a beast out of your Flock." "Content," said the Shepherd; and thereupon he went towards her, and she came towards him. He began to wrestle with her, but she immediately flung him, and took a beast out of the Flock, which she carried away with her into the Sea. She came afterwards every evening, and did the like, so that the Shepherd was head over heels in love with her. The Flock diminish'd, and the Shepherd himself pin'd away. One day King *Gebirus* passing by the Shepherd, found him sitting near his Flock very pensive, which obliged him to come nearer him, and to speak thus to him: "What misfortune hath befell thee? Why do I find thee so fallen away? The flock is so too, it diminishes and grows worse and worse every day, and gives less Milk than ordinarily it used to do." Thereupon the Shepherd told him the story of the young Lady. He was astonished at it, and said to him; "At what time does this Lady come thus to see thee?" "In the evening (reply'd the Shepherd) when the Sun is ready to set." Upon that *Gebirus* lighted off his Beast, and said to the Shepherd; "Take off thy Garment and strip thyself." The shepherd obey'd, and the King put on the Shepherds Garment, cloathed himself like him, and sate in his place. A little while after behold the young Lady, who was already come out of the Sea, comes to salute him. He returned the salute, and she said to him; "Wilt thou wrestle any more on the same terms we have done already?" "With all my heart," said the King. Immediately she came near him, and endeavoured to cast him down; but *Gebirus* gave her a fall presently, and violently crush'd her. Whereupon she said to him, "You are not my ordinary match." "No," said the King. "Since I cannot avoid being taken (said she) put me into the hands of my former match; for he has treated me courteously, and I have tormented his heart many times: meantime he hath captivated me as I have captivated him. In requital I will teach you the way to complete this Building, as you desire." After therefore he had put her into the hands of the Shepherd, he desired her to tell him whence came that which happened every day to his Building; and if there were any means to make it continue in that condition whereto they brought it. "There are," reply'd she; "but know, great Prince, that the Land of *Egypt* is a Land of Enchanters, and that the Sea there is full of Spirits and Demons, which assist them to carry on their affairs, and that they are those who take away your Buildings." "But what means is there to prevent it?" said the King. "To do that (said she) you shall make great Vessels of Transparent glass, with Covers thereto, which may keep the waters from entering in; and you shall put into them Men well-skill'd in Painting, and with them Meat and Drink for a week, and Cloaths, and Pencils, and whatever is necessary for Painting. Then you shall stop the Vessels well, after you have fastened them at the top with strong Cords, and ty'd them to the Ships, and then you shall let them go into the Sea like Anchors, and you shall put at the top of the cords little Bells, which the Painters shall ring; and then I will tell you what it is requisite that you should do." *Gebirus* did all she had ordered him; he caused the Vessels to be made, and brought the Painters before her, who heard all she said to him; then he promised them great wealth and honours, and they promised him to do his business. They therefore put these Vessels to the bottom of the Sea, after they had stopped them well above, and fastened them with cord, and left them there a week: after which the Painters rung the Bells, and presently they were taken out of the water, and they opened the Vessels, out of which they took away with them the Draughts they had made. The King presented them afterwards to the young lady *Marina*, and she said to them; "Make now Statues of Copper, and Tin, and Stone, and Earth, and Wood, resembling your Draughts, and set them on the Sea-side, before the Buildings you shall make: for then the Beasts of the Sea, when they shall come out to demolish your Buildings as they are wont, seeing those Figures, will imagine that they are companies of Demons like themselves, come to fight with them, and they will presently return to the place whence they came." The Painters and Gravers did so, and by that means *Gebirus* completed his Structure as he desired. . . .

By this means he completed the Building of the City, which coming to the knowledge of *Charoba*, she was very much displeased thereat, and fell into a great disturbance. For her intention was only to weary out the King, and to reduce him to an impossibility. . . . After *Gebirus* had acquitted himself of the Building of the City, he sent the tidings of it to *Charoba*, and invited her to come and see it. It was her Nurse who brought her the news, and withall said to her, "Fear not, nor give yourself any trouble concerning him." Then presently she carried to *Gebirus* a piece of Tapistry of great value, and said to him: "Put this on the Seat in which you shall sit, and afterwards divide your people into three parties, and send them to me that I may give them a Treatment such as they deserve. When the first party shall be about a third part of the way, you shall send away the second, then afterwards the third, to the end they may be near us dispersed in the Countrey for our safety." He did so, and in the mean time she continued sending to him precious Household-stuff, till such time as she knew that they were upon their way, and that he had sent to her the third part of his Army. Then she caused to be set for them Tables, replenish'd with Poisoned Meats and Drinks, and when they were come to the Tables, her Servants Men and Maids made them stay and sit down to eat, standing all about them with Umbrellos or Fans, so that they all died from the first to the last. They afterwards quitted that Post, and passed to the other, where the second party met them, whom they treated after the same manner. Then they removed to the third, and serv'd them as they had done the others, so that all died. After that she sent word to the King, that she had left his Army in her own City, and in her Castle and thereabouts, for the safety of Her Women; and that she would be served by his Attendants, who should be about him ready to obey him. Accordingly she went to his Palace, accompanied by her Nurse and some of her meaner Women, who were with her, and carried Perfumes in Porcelain Dishes. He rose up and went to meet her, and immediately her Nurse put about him a sumptuous Robe, but poisoned, which she had prepared for that purpose; and blew a Fume into his face, which in a like manner deprived him of his senses; then she sprinkled him with a water which she had, which loosened all his members, and dislocated all his joynts, so that he fell to the ground in a swound. Then she opened his veins, and emptied them of all his bloud, saying, The bloud of Kings is an excellent remedy. Her Nurse came up to him, and said to him; "Is the King well to night?" "Mischief on your coming hither, (replied he;) may you be treated accordingly." "Do you stand in need of any thing (replied she) before you taste death?" "I do, said he; I would intreat thee to cause these words to be engraved upon one of the pillars of the Castle: *I Gebirus the son of Gevirus the Mutaphequian, who have caused Marble to be polished, and the hard red stone and the green to be wrought; who have been possessed of Gold and Precious stones; who have built Palaces, and raised Armies; who have cut through Mountains, who have stopped Rivers with my arm: with all this my power, and my might, and my prowess, and my valour, I have been circumvented by the artifices of a Woman, weak, impotent, and of no worth; who hath deprived me of my understanding, and taken my life, and discomfited my Armies. Whoever therefore is desirous to prosper, though there be no prosperity in this world, let him have a care of the wilely subtilties of Women. This is the advice I give those who shall come after me. I have no more to say.*"[1]

---

1. In one form or another these tales also occur in the *Abridgement of Marvels* and other Arabic works. The 14th-century Ibn Khaldun refers to the story of the painted vessels as an example of the credulity of some historians.

From the "Thousand and One Nights"

The Three Walis

PROBABLY THE BEST known Arabic work in Europe is the collection of stories known as *The Thousand and one Nights*. First presented to the West in the French translation of Antoine Galland (twelve volumes, Paris, 1704–17), it has enjoyed perennial popularity, and many translations, good and bad, have appeared in almost all the languages of Europe.

The authorship, origin and date of the work have for long been subjects of dispute among Oriental scholars. The earliest references to the *Nights* in other books come from the tenth century—yet many of the stories cannot have been written earlier than the fourteenth or fifteenth century. Several different recensions of the collection are extant which by no means tally in the selection and arrangement of the tales. Within the framework of the story of Shahrazad, more familiar as Sheherazade, the collection has gradually grown through the centuries, each age and each country adding its own contribution and imparting something of itself to the book as a whole. Most of the late versions that have come down to us appear to have been edited in Egypt, where the *Nights* have for long enjoyed special popularity. Many of the tales themselves are of unmistakable Egyptian authorship and origin. Such masterpieces of Egyptian narrative literature as the story of Ma'ruf the cobbler and the story of Abu Kir and Abu Sir are unfortunately too long to be included here. The following brief tale of one of the Mamluk Sultans of Egypt and three of his governors is in the translation of E.W. Lane.

AL-MALIK AN-NASIR[1] summoned one day the three Walis, the Wali of Al-Qahira,[2] the Wali of Bulaq, and the Wali of Misr al-Qadima, and said, I desire that each of you acquaint me with the most wonderful thing that hath happened to him during the period of his holding the office of Wali. And they replied, We hear and obey.

Accordingly, the Wali of Al-Qahira said, Know, O our lord the Sultan, that the most wonderful thing that hath happened to me during the period of my holding the office of Wali was as follows: there were, in this city, two legal witnesses,[3] who gave testimony respecting blood and wounds; but they were addicted to the love of (disreputable) women, and the drinking of wine, and iniquity; and I could succeed in no stratagem to revenge myself upon them. So being unable to do this, I charged the vintners, and the sellers of dried fruits, and those of fresh fruits, and the dealers in candles, and the keepers of houses prepared for vicious practices, that they should inform me of these two witnesses whenever they might be in a place drinking, or committing any act of iniquity, whether they should be together or separate, and if they bought, or either of them bought, anything of these persons that was designed for the purpose of carousing; and that they should not conceal it from me. They replied, that they heard and obeyed. And it happened that a man came to me one night, and said, O our lord, know that the two witnesses are in such a place, in such a by-street, in the house of such-a-one, and that they are engaged in abominable iniquity. So I arose and disguised myself, I and my young man, and I repaired to them without anyone accompanying me save my young man, and

---

1. There were several Sultans of Egypt thus surnamed. E.W.L.

2. Cairo; now commonly called by its inhabitants "Masr," for "Misr." Bulaq is the principal port of Cairo. Misr al-Qadima, "Old Misr," now commonly called by the Egyptians Masr al-'Atiqa, which has the same meanings; and by Europeans, improperly, "Old Cairo." E.W.L.

3. A "legal witness" was a kind of notary.

stopped not on the way until I stood before the door and knocked; whereupon a female slave came to me and opened to me the door, and said, Who art thou? So I entered without answering her; and I beheld the two witnesses and the master of the house sitting, with common women, and with abundance of wine. But when they saw me, they rose to me, treated me with honor, seated me at the upper end of the apartment, and said to me, Welcome to thee, as an excellent guest, and a polite boon-companion! They met me without fearing me or being alarmed; and after that, the master of the house arose from them, and having been absent a while, returned bringing three hundred pieces of gold, without the least fear; and they said, Know, O our lord the Wali, that thou cannot do more than disgrace us, and that it is in thy power to chastise us; but naught save fatigue would accrue to thee from doing so. It is advisable, therefore, that thou receive this sum, and protect us; for God (whose name be exalted!) is named the Excellent Protector, and He loveth of his servants such as are liberal of protection; and thou wilt receive a reward and recompense.—So I said to myself, Receive this gold from them, and protect them this time; and if thou have them in thy power another time, take thy revenge upon them. I coveted the money, and took it from them, and left them and departed, no one knowing what I had done. But suddenly on the following day a sergeant of the Qadi came to me, and said, O Wali, have the goodness to answer the summons of the Qadi for he citeth thee. I arose, therefore, and went with him to the Qadi, not knowing the cause of this; and when I went in to him, I saw the two witnesses and the master of the house who gave me the three hundred pieces of gold sitting with him; and the master of the house arose and sued for three hundred pieces of gold. It was not in my power to deny it; and he produced a written obligation, and those two legal witnesses testified against me that I owed the money. So it was established with the Qadi by the testimony of the two witnesses, and he ordered me to pay that sum. I therefore went not forth from them until they had received from me the three hundred pieces of gold; and I was enraged, purposing every kind of mischief against them, and repenting that I had not tormented them; and I departed in a state of the utmost confusion.

Then rose the Wali of Bulaq, and said, As to myself, O our lord the Sultan, the most wonderful thing that hath happened to me since I have been Wali was this:—I had debts to pay amounting to three hundred thousand pieces of gold; and, being distressed thereby I sold what was behind me and what was before me and what was in my hand, and thus collected one hundred thousand pieces of gold and no more. I therefore remained in great perplexity; and while I was sitting in my house one night, in this state, a person knocked at the door; upon which I said to one of the young men, See who is at the door. And he went forth, and then returned to me with sallow countenance, changed in complexion, and with the muscles of his side quivering. So I said to him, What hath befallen thee? And he answered, Verily at the door is a man stripped of his proper clothing, and clad in apparel of leather, and with a sword, and in his girdle is a knife, and with him is a party of men equipped in the same manner, and he asketh for thee. I therefore took my sword in my hand, and went forth to see who these were; and, lo, they were as the young man had said. I asked them, What is your affair? And they answered, We are robbers, and we have acquired this night vast booty, and assigned it to thee, that thou mayest thereby help thyself to manage the affair on account of which thou art in anxiety, and pay the debt that thou owest. I said to them, And where is the booty? And they brought before me a great chest of vessels (apparently) of gold and silver. So when I beheld it, I rejoiced, and said within myself, I will pay the debt that I owe from this, and there will remain to me as much again as the amount of that debt. I therefore took it, and entered the house, and said within myself, It would not be consistent with humanity in me to let them go without anything. Accordingly, I took the hundred thousand pieces of gold that were in my possession, and gave it to them, thanking them for what they had done; and they took the pieces of gold and went their way under the covering of night, without anyone knowing of their coming. But when the morning arrived, I saw that the contents of the chest were gilded brass, and tin, the whole of them worth but five hundred pieces of silver; and the thing afflicted me; the pieces of gold that I had were lost; and my grief was increased.

Then the Wali of Misr al-Qadima arose and said, O our lord the Sultan, with regard to myself, the most wonderful thing that hath happened to me during the period of my holding the office of Wali was this:—I hanged ten robbers, each on a separate gallows, and charged the guards to watch them, and not to suffer the people to take away any one of them. But on the morrow I came to see them, and beheld two men hanged upon one gallows; so I said to the guards, Who did this, and where is the gallows on which was the second of these hanged men? They however denied the fact; and I was about to beat them, when they said, Know, O Amir, that we slept last night, and when we awoke, we found that one hanged man had been stolen, together with the gallows on which he was suspended; whereupon we feared thee; and, lo, a peasant on a journey approached us, having with him an ass; and we seized him and killed him, and hanged him instead of the one that was stolen, on this gallows. And I wondered at this, and said to them, What was with the peasant? They answered, With him was a pair of saddle-bags on the ass.—And what, said I, was in them? They answered, We know not. And I said to them, Bring me the saddle-bags. So they placed them before me; and I gave orders to open them; and, lo, in them was a murdered man, cut in pieces; and when I saw this, I wondered at it, and said within myself, Extolled be the perfection of God! The cause of the hanging of this peasant was naught but the crime that he had committed against this murdered man; and thy Lord is not tyrannical towards his servants!

IN 1883 THE ORIENTALIST Wilhelm Spitta Bey published a collection of Egyptian folk tales under the title *Contes Arabes Modernes*. With one exception (not included here), the tales were related to him by his cook Hassan, whom he describes in these words: "He cannot read or write, but is intelligent and possesses an excellent memory. With this quality, he has retained since childhood all the stories told him by his mother, his aunts and old women who visited his parents' house." Spitta took down the stories as told him, in the dialect of Lower Egypt, and published them in a phonetic transcription with a French translation.

The Story of Dalal

THERE WAS ONCE a king who had a little daughter called Dalal. One day she sat scratching her hair and she found a little louse. She looked at it a while and then went to the pantry and put it in a jar of oil and sealed it. The louse remained there until Dalal grew up and reached the age of twenty. Then the louse burst the jar

by its size and came out like a buffalo with horns. The steward left
the pantry and called the servants. They surrounded the louse,
seized it and led it before the king. He asked them what it was.
Dalal was standing by him, and she said: "It is my louse, O my
father. When I was a little girl I was scratching my head and found
it in my hair. I put it in a jar of oil, and when it grew it burst the jar."
The king said to her: "You need a husband, my daughter. The louse
has burst the jar. Tomorrow you too will jump over the walls and go
to men. It is better that you should be married now."

So the king called the vizier and said to him: "Slaughter the louse
and hang its hide by the gate; take with you the executioner and the
holy man who will draw up the marriage contract. Whoever shall
know the skin as that of a louse, him shall you marry to Dalal, and
if anyone does not know it, cut off his head and impale it on the
gate." The vizier stripped off the skin of the louse and hung it by the
gate. Then he sent a crier through the town, saying: "Whoever shall
know the skin that hangs by the gate shall marry the king's daughter." The people of the city gathered round the palace gates. Some
of them said: "This is the skin of a buffalo," and others said: "This
is the skin of an ox," until the heads of forty men less one had been
cut off.

A little later an ogre passed by in the form of a man. He said to
the people: "What is this crowd?" They told him: "Whoever knows
this skin shall marry the king's daughter." The ogre went to the
vizier and said to him: "I shall name this skin to you." The vizier
said: "Speak," and he answered: "It is the skin of a louse swollen in
oil." They said to him: "It is true, O wise one. Come, make the marriage contract in the presence of the king." The ogre went before
the king. They wrote the contract and celebrated the wedding feast
until the ogre went in to his bride.

The ogre stayed with her for forty days in the king's palace; then
he went to the king and said: "I am the son of a king and a sultan. I
wish to take my wife and go, to return to the palace of my father and
dwell there." The king replied: "It is well, my son. Tomorrow we
shall prepare for you presents and slave-girls and eunuchs." The
ogre said: "We have many of those. I want nothing but my wife."

The king said: "It is well; take her and go. But take her mother with her that she may know where she lives." The ogre replied: "Why should we trouble her mother? Once every month I will bring her home to you!" The ogre took her and went.

He led her to his house and left her there. Then he went to the mountains, took on his true shape and brought her the head of a mortal man, saying: "Take it, Dalal, cut up his head and eat it." She replied: "It is the head of a man, and I eat only the flesh of sheep." The ogre went and brought her a sheep. She cooked it and ate some. When eight days had passed the ogre went and changed himself into the shape of her mother. He put on the garb of a woman and knocked at the door. Dalal looked through the window and asked: "Who knocks at the door?" The ogre replied: "Open, my daughter; it is I, your mother." Dalal went down and opened the door. As soon as he saw her he said: "How are you, my daughter? I heard that your husband is an ogre who feeds you on human flesh. I fear for you lest he eat you. Come, flee with me." She replied: "Be silent, my mother. Do not speak such words. He is the son of a king as I am the daughter of a king. His treasures are far greater than the treasures of my father." The ogre left her and went, his heart full of joy because she had not revealed his secret. He brought her a sheep and said: "Take it and cook it, Dalal, and eat." She said: "My mother was here; she greets you." He said: "If only I had hurried I might have met her. Tomorrow I shall send your mother's sister for you to see." The next morning at daybreak the ogre took on the shape of her mother's sister. He put on the garb of a woman and knocked at the door. Dalal asked: "Who is there?" And he answered: "Open; it is your aunt. Your mother sent me to see you." She went down and opened the door, and the ogre kissed her cheeks and wept and said: "O my daughter, I hear that your husband is an ogre." Dalal answered: "Be silent, do not speak such words, he is the son of a king and a sultan. Come and see his treasures upstairs." They went upstairs together and Dalal laid the table and brought food. So she dined and left. The ogre was pleased and came back with a sheep. She told him: "My aunt came and greets you," and he said: "Your relatives come, and yet I do not see them.

I shall send your father's sister to see you, Dalal, for I hear that she is dear to you."

When eight days more had passed the ogre changed himself into the shape of her aunt, her father's sister. He put on the garb of a woman and knocked at the door. "Who is there?" asked Dalal. "Open, my child; it is I, your aunt." Dalal went down and opened he door. The ogre kissed her and said: "O my child, I hear that your husband is an ogre." Then Dalal wept and said: "Be silent, O my aunt. He brings me the heads of men and tells me to cut them up and cook them. I fear lest he eat me." The ogre resumed his own shape. When Dalal saw him she was terrified. He said to her: "Do you thus reveal my secret, Dalal?" She said: "Forgive me." He said: "You have dishonored me. Tell me, where does your food come from?" Dalal said: "Will you eat me unwashed as I am? The taste of my flesh will be unpleasant in your mouth. Take me to the bath where I shall cleanse and perfume myself. When I come out you shall eat me as it may please you." The ogre said: "You speak truth, Dalal."

He brought her a bath-ewer and the finest of clothes and sought out another ogre, whom he changed into a white mule. He changed himself into a groom, put the ewer on his head, mounted her on the mule and led her to the place of the bath. There he took her by the hand to the woman who kept the bath and said to her: "Take these three mahbubs[1] and tend the lady, the wife of the king, in her bath; as I have entrusted her to you so shall you return her to me." He left her and waited by the door of the bath.

Dalal went in and sat on a bench; while the young girls entered, bathed and went out joyously, playing with one another, Dalal sat on a bench and wept. The young girls said to her: "What ails you, sister? Why do you weep? Come, disrobe, and bathe with us." She replied: "There is still plenty of time to bathe."

Soon there came an old woman selling lupine, with a tray of lupine on her head. Dalal called her and said: "Give me lupine for twenty paras." The lupine-seller came near and sat by her. Dalal

---

1. "Beloved"—the common Egyptian name of the Turkish gold sequin.

said: "O my aunt!" She answered: "Yes, my daughter." Dalal said: "Will you give me this tray of lupine and the tattered garments that you wear in exchange for this golden ewer and my jewels and garments? You put them on and I will put on yours." The old woman replied: "Because you are rich, do you mock one who is poor?" Dalal said: "I speak true words to you, O aged mother." Then the old woman took off her garments, exchanged them for those of Dalal and, rejoicing, left by the main door of the baths. Dalal soiled her face and hands with the mud on the floor of the bath; then she put the tray of lupine on her head and went out, trembling with fear, by the door where the ogre sat. She cried: "Roast lupine, who will buy, roast lupine!"

When the ogre saw her, he smelt her and recognized her. He said: "Is it she or not?" He hastened to the woman who kept the baths and said: "Where is the lady, the wife of the king, whom I entrusted to you?" She replied: "She is within, bathing with the young women." He said: "Why does she delay?" She answered: "Soon they will come out. They do not leave until evening approaches." The ogre was appeased and sat by the door until all the young women had left the baths. The attendant came out among them and locked the doors. The ogre asked her: "Where is the lady whom I entrusted to you?" She answered: "Has she not already returned to you?" "No, she has not returned. I demand that you give her back to me as I gave her to you." The attendant replied: "Go seek her at home. If she has lost a jewel or a garment, I am answerable for it. I am a keeper of clothes and not a keeper of women." The ogre left her and went his way. He was filled with a great anger and said: "By God, though she be in the seventh world I will follow her till I find her and devour her."

When Dalal left the bath she tried to return to her own land, but went astray on the road. She found a watercourse where she washed her face and feet. Then she went on walking until she came to the palace of a certain king. She sat down by the palace walls. A black slave-girl who came down to clean the linen saw her and went to her mistress, saying: "Were it not for my fear and terror of you, I would say, my lady, that there is one below more beautiful than you." Her mistress replied: "It is well. Go, summon her to me." The slave-girl went to Dalal and said: "Come, speak with my mistress." Dalal replied: "Was my mother a slave-girl or my father a slave that I should go up with slave-girls?" The slave-girl went and told her mistress what Dalal had said to her. She sent a white slave-girl, saying: "Go, call her." The white slave-girl went to her and said: "Come, my lady, speak with my mistress above." Dalal answered: "I am not a white slave-girl that I should go up with slave-girls." The white slave-girl went and told her mistress what Dalal had said. Then the lady called her son, the prince, and said to him: "Go, call the lady who is below." He went to Dalal and said: "Deign to enter the harem," and she answered: "Now I shall come, for you are the son of a king as I am the daughter of a king," and she went with him up the stairs.

No sooner had the prince seen her walking up the stairs than love for her entered his heart. As soon as the lady, the wife of the king, saw her, she said to herself: "The words of the slave-girl are true; she is indeed more beautiful than I." The prince said to his mother: "I wish to marry her, for it is clear that she is a daughter of kings." His mother answered: "My son, I fear lest she be an ogress in human form who, when you lie with her in bed, will rise in the night and eat you and then turn upon us and eat us." He said: "Do not speak such words, my mother, for I know that she is a king's daughter as I am a king's son." His mother answered: "You know what is best for you, my son." He summoned the Qadi, drew up the marriage deed and ordered the celebration of the wedding.

Now the ogre raged through the land seeking Dalal. In each place he stayed for a day or two until at last he reached the prince's palace where Dalal dwelt. He saw the preparations for the wedding feast and asked one of the servants: "Whose feast is this?" The servant said: "This is for the son of the king who is marrying a certain king's daughter that he found wandering in the street." The ogre went and called another ogre, to whom he said: "Change yourself into human shape and I shall take the shape of a large white sheep. Go to the king and say to him: 'O king, here is a gift from me. But do not leave it below, tether it in the women's quarters, for I have reared it among the women. And if you tether it below it will bleat all night and let no one sleep.'"

The ogre took the sheep and went. He found the king standing. As soon as the king saw the sheep he liked it and said: "Are you selling this sheep, O sheikh?" He answered: "I bring it to you as a gift without money," and he spoke as the ogre had told him. The king said: "It is well," and gave it to a eunuch to take to the bride for her to see. The eunuch took it upstairs and tethered it by the bride's door.

Now this was the bridal night. The prince went in to her and slept with her in the bed. When he was asleep the ogre broke his tether and entered the chamber. He seized Dalal and carried her to the anteroom, saying: "Tell me Dalal, where does your food come from?" She answered: "From your honor." He said: "Have you left me any honor? I have suffered long enough on your account." She said: "Be patient one moment while I go to the privy to relieve a need." Dalal went to the privy, while the ogre held the door and waited for her. She said: "O Lady Zaynab,[2] who help the young in their misfortunes!" The Lady Zaynab sent one of her sisters of the company of the Jinn. She clove the wall, came to her and said: "Why do you summon me, my daughter?" Dalal replied: "There is an ogre outside, O my Lady, who seeks to eat me." The Jinniya said: "If I kill him, will you promise to give me the first child you bear?" Dalal said: "It is well, my Lady." The Jinniya gave her a piece of wood and said: "When you go out the ogre will at once open his mouth to eat you. When he does so, throw this piece of wood straight into his mouth. He will fall in a faint. You can then call the servants to dispatch him." Dalal listened to her words and went out. The ogre opened his mouth to eat her. She threw the piece of wood in his mouth, and he fell to the ground in a faint. She ran to the prince, wakened him and said: "Come, kill the ogre who has come to eat us." The prince drew his sword, ran into the ante-room and cut the ogre in pieces. Then he and Dalal went back to bed and slept.

---

2. The daughter of 'Ali and granddaughter of the prophet. Her reputed birthday is still one of the major popular festivals of Egypt.

Dalal lived happily in the palace until she conceived and bore a child. Then the Jinniya clove the wall and came to her and said: "Give me the daughter that you have born." Dalal said: "Here she is; take her." She took her and went.

In the morning the king's mother came with her women to congratulate Dalal on the birth. The king's mother said: "Show me the child." Dalal wept and said: "I have no child." Then the prince's mother said: "It is even as I told you; she is an ogress; she has borne a child and eaten it. Only through fear of us did she refrain from eating one of us." They went to the prince and told him: "Your wife is an ogress, she has eaten her child." He said: "Take her to the kitchen and let her peel onions with the slave-girls."

The servants took her to the kitchen and she stayed there for ten years, peeling onions. Then the Jinniya clove the wall and said to her: "Here is your daughter, take her. Now she is grown and marriageable. I saw that you were afflicted and it grieved me. When the king enters his carriage, send forth your daughter and let her stand by the legs of his horses. The king will see her and ask: 'Whose daughter are you?' She will answer: 'I am your daughter.' He will say: 'Come, show me where your mother is,' so he will find you and take you back and you will be happier than before." The Jinniya left her and went. When day came Dalal sent her daughter to the gate as the king came out to ride. The little girl ran bare-headed before the legs of the horses. When the king saw her, he cried: "Stop, coachman," and said to her: "Whose daughter are you?" She answered: "Come, let me show you my mother." She walked before him and he followed until they reached the kitchen. She said: "There is my mother, sitting and peeling onions." The king took her, kissed her cheeks and carried her off on his shoulders. He ordered the servants to heat the bath. Then Dalal bathed and they dressed her in royal garments and she lived in the palace more happily than before.

When the Jinniya had gone the Sultan of the Jinn sent for her and asked: "Where is the girl whom you were rearing?" She answered: "I have returned her to her mother." He asked: "Can you not bring her back?" She said: "Why do you want her?" He answered: "My son is ill. The physician has said that he can only be healed by a goblet of water from the Emerald Sea, and that only a daughter of mortal man can bring it. Go please, bring her for an hour, and then you shall take her back." The Jinniya went and clove the wall and said: "O Dalal, give me your daughter for an hour. I shall bring her back to you." She said: "It is well, my Lady. Here she is. Take her." She took her and led her to the Sultan of the Jinn. As soon as the Sultan of the Jinn saw her, he gave her a goblet and said: "Take this and mount this Jinni. He will bear you to the Emerald Sea; fill this goblet from its waters." She said, "It is well," and mounted the Jinni who bore her to the Emerald Sea. She alighted to fill the goblet, but a sudden wave splashed her hand, which became as green as clover leaves. She remounted the Jinni and he carried her back. She gave the goblet to the Sultan of the Jinn, and the Jinniya, who was sitting there, took her back to her parents' home.

Now there is a weigher of the Sea of Emerald who weighs it every morning to see if anyone has stolen any. That morning he weighed it and found it short by one pound. He said: "Who has taken it? I shall go in search of him until I find him. If he has on his hand the mark of the Sea of Emerald I shall take him to the Sultan of the Sea. He will know what to do." He took bracelets and rings, put them on a tray and placed it on his head. He walked by the palaces, crying: "I have bracelets and rings, O young girls."

He went through the land until he came to the city where lived Dalal, and cried his wares. The king's daughter saw him from the window and said to her mother: "I want rings and bracelets. There is a man standing by the gate who is selling them." Dalal said "It is well, my daughter. Send the servant to fetch some." She answered: "No, I shall go and try them on my hands." Dalal said: "It is well. Go." She stretched out her left hand to the man by the gate. He said: "Are you not ashamed to give me your left hand?" But the girl was unwilling to show him her right hand, because of its color. She said: "My right hand hurts." He answered: "I need but to see it with my eyes, and I shall know the measure." As soon as the guardian of the Sea of Emerald saw it, he seized her by the hand and plunged with her into the earth. He led her to the servants of the Sea of

Emerald, saying: "Here is the one who stole the pound." They seized her and began to beat her with goblets. The Jinn gathered round her and parried the blows with their hands so that they did not reach her. Then the Sultan of the Sea of Emerald said: "Lead her to the baths and bind her hands. I shall change myself into a serpent and go there and devour her." They bound her hands and the Sultan of the Sea of Emerald went to her in the shape of a serpent. As soon as the girl saw him she said: "In the name of God! God's will be done! Were it not for the fear and terror which you inspire in me, I would say that your eyes are like the Sea of Emerald." The serpent replied: "Have you recognized me? Then you are of my women and I am of your men." He changed himself into human shape and said to her: "This night I shall lead you back to your father. I shall draw up the marriage contract with you and celebrate the wedding feast. And when I come to you by night, I shall come in the form of a flying serpent. I shall enter by the window and I shall leave by the window." He called the weigher of the Sea of Emerald and said: "Take the girl back where you found her." He took her back. The Sultan followed her, and went to her father and said: "I seek alliance with you by your daughter." The king replied: "It is well. Fix the marriage portion." He said: "The marriage portion shall be forty camels laden with emeralds and with hyacinths."

The drew up the marriage contract and celebrated the wedding feast for exactly forty days, and they lived happily ever after.

The Story of 'Arab-Zandiq

THERE WAS ONCE a king who said to his vizier: "Let us go and take a walk in the town by night." They walked and came upon a house where people were talking by night. They stood near and heard a woman say: "If the king marries me I will make him a pancake big enough for him and his army." A second woman said: "If the king marries me I will make him a tent big enough for him and his army." Then a third one said: "If the king marries me I will bear him a daughter and a son with alternate hairs of gold and hyacinth. If they cry it will thunder and the rain will fall and if they laugh the sun and the moon will rise." The king heard their words and walked away. When day broke he sent for the three of them and drew up the contract of marriage with them. On the first night he slept with the first and said to her: "Where is the pancake big enough for me and my army?" She answered: "The words of the night are greased with butter. When day rises they melt." On the second night he slept with the second and said to her: "Where is the tent big enough for me and my army?" She said: "It was a word that came to my mind." He ordered them both to the kitchen with the slave-girls. On the third night he slept with the youngest, and said to her: "Where are the son and the daughter with alternate hairs of gold and hyacinth?" She said: "Be patient with me for nine months and nine minutes."

She conceived and the nine months and nine minutes passed by. On the night when she was to give birth they sent for the midwife. But the king's other wife went and met her on the way and said to her: "When you deliver her child, how much will the king give you?" She answered: "He will command that they give me fifteen mahbubs." She said to her: "Take these forty mahbubs from me and take these two blind dogs. When she gives birth to the son and daughter take them away and put them in a casket and put these two dogs in their place. Take away the children and kill them." The midwife took the money and went, and when the children were born she took them away, placed them in a casket and put the two dogs in their place. Then she went to the king and said to him: "I am afraid to tell you." He said: "Tell me. I give you protection." She said: "She has borne two dogs." Then the king said: "Take her, cover her with pitch and tie her to the stairs, and whoever goes up and whoever goes down will spit on her." They took her and tied her to the staircase. The old midwife took away the children in the casket and went to throw it in the river. Now there was a fisherman who lived with his wife on an island, and his wife had borne no issue. The fisherman went down in the morning to fish, and he found the casket thrown on to the bank. He took it and went to his wife and put it between them and said to her: "Listen, O woman. I shall make a pact with you. If this is money it is my portion, and if it is children it is your portion." She said: "It is well. I am satisfied with this." They opened the casket and found the boy and the girl. The boy had put his finger in the girl's mouth and the girl had put her finger in the boy's mouth, and they were sucking one another's fingers. The woman picked them up and took them out of the casket, and prayed to her Lord: "Send me milk into my breasts for the sake of these children." By the power of the Almighty the milk

came into her breasts. She reared them until they grew up and
were twelve years old. The fisherman went down to fish and he
caught two large white fish. The boy said to him: "These two white
fish are beautiful, my father. I will take them to sell or to give them
as a gift to the king." The boy took them and went and sat in the
fish-market. The people gathered around him. Those who were not
looking at the fish were looking at the boy. The king passed that
way and saw the two white fish and the boy, and called out to him:
"How much are those?" He answered: "For you, nothing." The king
took him to the palace and said to him: "What is your name?" He
said: "My name is Muhammad and my father is the fisherman who
lives in the middle of the island." The king gave the boy thirty mahbubs, and said to him: "Go, clever one, and come back here every
day."

The boy went and gave his father the thirty mahbubs. The next
day he took the fish and went to give them to the king. The king
took them, went into the garden with him and made him sit by him.
The king sat drinking wine and looking at the beauty of the boy.
Love for the boy entered his heart, and he stayed with him for two
hours. Then he ordered a horse for him to ride when he came and
went to the king. He mounted the horse and rode away. The next
day he came to the king and sat with him in the garden. The king's
wife looked out of the window and saw the boy, and knew him. She
sent for the old woman and said to her: "I told you to kill those children. They are still living on the face of the earth." She answered:
"Be patient with me, O Queen, for three days, and I will kill him."
The old woman went and bought a pitcher. She bound a sash round
it and bewitched it. Then she mounted it and struck it with a whip.
The pitcher flew with her and alighted on the island by the fisherman's hut. She met the girl, the sister of clever Muhammad, sitting
alone, and said to her: "O my daughter, why do you sit alone and so
unhappy? Tell your brother to bring you the rose of 'Arab-Zandiq,
to stay with you and sing to you and amuse you instead of sitting
alone and so unhappy." The old woman said these words and left
her. When her brother came to her, he found her unhappy and said:
"Why are you so unhappy, my sister?" She said: "I want the rose of

'Arab-Zandiq to sing to me and amuse me." He answered: "I am ready. I will bring it to you."

He mounted his horse and traveled far into the mountain. He met an ogress sitting and grinding corn with a handmill. He dismounted from his horse and found her breasts thrown back over her shoulders. He drank from her right breast and from her left breast, and came before her and said: "Peace be with you, O Mother ogress." She said: "Had not your greeting preceded your words I would have eaten your flesh before your bones. Where are you going, O clever Muhammad?" He said: "I am going to bring the singing rose of 'Arab-Zandiq." She showed him the way and said to him: "You will come to a palace before which a goat and a dog are tethered. Before the goat is meat and before the dog is clover. Take the meat from before the goat and throw it before the dog; take the clover and throw it before the goat. Then the gate will open for you and you will go in and pick the rose. Then go out at once and do not look back, for if you do you will be bewitched and turned to stone like the other ones who have been bewitched in that place." The clever Muhammad went and did as the ogress had told him. He picked the rose and went out of the gate, put back the meat before the goat and the clover before the dog. He carried off the rose and gave it to his sister. Then he went to the king again. The king greeted him and said: "Where have you been, O clever one? Why have you been away from me so long?" He answered: "I was ill, O king." He took him and went into the garden with him, and they sat together. The king's wife looked out of the window and saw them sitting together. She sent for the old woman and struck her a violent blow and said: "Are you laughing at me, old woman?" She answered: "Be patient with me for three days more." She mounted her pitcher and went to the girl and said to her: "Did your brother bring you the rose?" She answered: "Yes, but it does not sing." The old woman said: "It only sings before its mirror," and she went away.

When her brother came he found her unhappy, and said to her: "Why are you unhappy, my sister?" She said: "I want the mirror of the rose, without which it will not sing." He said: "It is well. I am ready. I will bring it to you." He mounted his horse and went to the ogress. She asked: "What do you want, O clever Muhammad?" He said: "I want the mirror of the rose." She said: "It is well. Do as you did last time with the dog and the goat. When you go into the garden you will find a staircase. Go up the stairs and in the first room you will find the mirror hanging on the wall. Take it and go out at once and do not look back. If the earth trembles while you are there, make your heart hard; otherwise you will have gone in vain." The clever Muhammad went as the ogress had told him and took the mirror. The earth trembled, but he made his heart as hard as an anvil and its trembling did not trouble him.

He carried off the mirror and gave it to his sister. She put it by the rose, but the rose did not sing. He went to the king, who said to him: "Where have you been, O clever one?" He said: "I was away with my father traveling somewhere; now I have come back." The king took him and went into the garden. The king's wife saw him and sent for the old woman and said to her: "Are you laughing at me, old woman?" She answered: "Be patient with me for three days more, O Queen. This time it will be the beginning and the end." Then she mounted her pitcher and went to the girl and said to her: "Did your brother bring you the mirror?" She answered: "Yes, but the rose does not sing." She said: "It only sings with its mistress, whose name is 'Arab-Zandiq." Then she left her and went away. The boy went and found his sister unhappy. He asked her: "Why are you unhappy, my sister?" She answered: "I want 'Arab-Zandiq, the mistress of the rose and the mirror, so that they may sing to me and I may take pleasure in them when I sit alone." He mounted his horse and went to the ogress and said to her: "How are you, mother ogress?" She said: "What else do you want, O clever Muhammad?" He answered: "I want 'Arab-Zandiq, the mistress of the rose and the mirror." She said: "O clever Muhammad, kings and pashas were not able to bring her, and they were all bewitched and turned into stone. You are still young and poor and what will happen to you?" He said: "Just show me the way, O mother ogress, and I will bring her with the permission of God." She said: "Go to the west of the palace and you will find an open window. Put your horse's head against the wall and shout with all your might and say to her: 'Come down, O 'Arab-Zandiq!'" The clever Muhammad went and stood beneath the window. He put the horse's head against the window and shouted: "Come down, O 'Arab-Zandiq!" She looked out and cursed him and said: "Go away, O youth." The clever Muhammad looked and saw that half of the horse had turned to stone. He shouted again with all his might: "Come down, O 'Arab-Zandiq!" She cursed him and said: "I told you to go away, O youth." He looked and saw that his horse was bewitched and half of himself too. He shouted again with all his might and said: "I told you to come down, O 'Arab-Zandiq!" She leaned half out of the window, and her hair reached the ground. The clever Muhammad seized her hair, rolled it round his hand, pulled her and threw her on to the ground. She said: "You are destined for me, O clever Muhammad. Let go my hair, by the life of the king your father." He said to her: "My father is not a king; my father is a fisherman." She said: "No, your father is the king, and later I will tell you his story." He said: "I will not let go your hair until you set free all these bewitched men." She made a sign with her right hand and they were set free. They came rushing to the clever Muhammad, wishing to take her from him. But some of them said: "Thanks be to him who saved us. Do you wish to take her from him?" So they left him and went away. She took him and went into her castle and ordered her servants to go and build a palace in the middle of the fisherman's island. The servants went and built the palace. She took the clever Muhammad and she and her army departed. She said to him: "Go to the king, and when he asks you where you have been, say: 'I am arranging my wedding, and you and your army are invited.'" The clever Muhammad went to the king, who said to him: "Where have you been, O clever one?" He answered: "I was preparing for my wedding, and I have come to invite you and all your army." The king laughed and said to the vizier: "This boy is the son of a fisherman, and he comes to invite me and my army." The vizier said: "For the sake of your love for him, let us command the army to take eight days' food with them, and we too will take our food." The king ordered them to prepare the army with eight days' food, and they went to the fisher-

man's son. The army found fine tents raised. The king was astonished. Then food was brought to them, cakes and meat, and as soon
as the dish before them was finished another one was brought. The
soldiers said to one another: "If only we could stay here for two
years and eat meat instead of eating beans and lentils!" They stayed
for exactly forty days until the wedding was over, and they were
well content with the food. The king and his army went, and he said
to the vizier: "We would like to invite them as they have invited
us"—and he sent them an invitation. 'Arab-Zandiq sent her soldiers,
and they filled the town until no place was found for them, and they
were scattered amongst the peasants so that they might be fed.
Then 'Arab-Zandiq went with the girl and the clever Muhammad,
and they entered the palace. As they were going up the stairs 'Arab-
Zandiq saw the mother of the clever Muhammad coated with pitch
and shackled. She threw a cashmere shawl over her and covered
her. The servants who were standing there asked her: "Why do you
cover her with the shawl? Spit on her when you go up and again
when you come down." She asked them why. They said: "Because
she bore the king two dogs." The servants went and brought news
to the king, saying: "A lady of the guests had thrown a shawl over
the one who stands by the stairs. She covered her and does not spit
on her." The king met her and asked: "Why did you cover her?" She
said: "Let her be taken to the baths and cleansed and dressed in
royal clothes and later I will tell you her story."

The king gave orders and they took her to the baths and
cleansed her and dressed her in royal clothes. Then they led her
before them in the divan. The king said to 'Arab-Zandiq: "Now tell
me her story." She said: "Listen, O king, and the fisherman will
speak." Then 'Arab-Zandiq asked the fisherman: "Did your wife
bear the clever Muhammad and his sister at one time or separately?" The fisherman answered: "My wife has borne no children." She
said: "Then where did you get them?" He answered: "I went down
one morning to fish, and I found them in a casket in the river. I took
them and my wife reared them." 'Arab-Zandiq said: "Do you hear, O
king?" He said to the woman: "Are these your children, woman?"
She said: "Let them bare their heads, that I may see." The children

bared their heads and they found alternate hairs of gold and hya-cinth. Then the king asked: "Are these your children?" She said: "Let them weep. If it thunders and rains they are my children, but if it does not thunder or rain they are not my children." The children wept and it thundered and rained. They said to her: "Are these your children?" She said: "Let them laugh. If the moon rises with the sun they are my children." The children laughed, and the moon rose with the sun. They said to her: "Are these your children?" She answered: "They are my children and the issue of my womb." Then the king gave orders and made the fisherman his vizier of the right hand and ordered that the city be illuminated for exactly forty days. On the last day he brought his wife and the old midwife. He had them burnt in fire and scattered to the winds.

From Modern Egypt

'Amm Mitwalli

Mahmud Taimur Bey was born in 1894, in Darb Sa'ada, a district of old Cairo. He came of a prominent family of Turkish origin, whose members included a number of distinguished scholars and writers. He was much influenced in his youth by his father, Ahmad Taimur Pasha, a well-known scholar and littérateur, and his brother Muhammad, himself a story-writer of distinction. Later he studied European and especially French literature, and himself names Maupassant as one who exercised a decisive influence on his literary development. He published many volumes of short stories and was generally recognized as the leading Arabic short-story writer of his time. He died in 1973. *'Amm Mitwalli*, one of his earlier works, was first published in 1925 and reissued in a completely revised version in 1942. It deals with the age-old belief in the "Mahdi," the "rightly guided one," a Messianic personage who, according to Muslim tradition, will in due time be sent by God "to cleanse the world of its corruption" and to inaugurate an era of justice and purified Islam. There have been many pretenders to the title of Mahdi in Islamic history, whose activities had far-reaching moral and material effects. Among these was Muhammad Ahmad, the Mahdi of the Sudan, whose career, beginning in 1881, culminated in the creation of an independent

163

Muslim state in the Sudan, free from Egyptian or British control. It was destroyed in 1898, when an Anglo-Egyptian force, commanded by Lord Kitchener, defeated the forces of the Mahdi's heir and successor and captured his capital of Khartoum.

The following is translated from the 1942 edition.

'Amm Mitwalli was a hawker of peanuts, melon seeds and sweets, well known to the inhabitants of Hilmiya and the neighboring districts. He went about in a long white turban and a broad-sleeved *gallabiya*,[1] with a dignified demeanour, and cried his wares to the children with a Sudanese accent, in a faltering voice weakened by poverty and infirmity, yet still retaining something of the ring of command.

The man had grown up in the Sudan and had fought in the armies of the Mahdi with the rank of Divisional Commander. He had lived all his life alone, with neither wife nor child; and occupied a small, dark room in the alley of 'Abdallah Bey, furnished only with an old trunk and a straw mat with a tattered cushion and blanket. Yet despite his obvious and abject poverty, cleanliness encompassed him and all he possessed.

He used to return to his room overwhelmed with weariness. When he had recited the evening prayer he would light his pallid oil lamp, sit by his trunk and take out an old sword. He would rest it across his knees and sink into long reveries, going over the memories of his past life; and when the memory of the Mahdi passed through his mind he would lift up his eyes and pray to God to hasten the days of Return, the days of the awaited reappearance of the Mahdi,—the Flagbearer of the Faith—when he would descend upon the world and cleanse it of its corruptions. Then he would lower his eyes, stroke his tear-stained beard, and take the old sword and kiss it with great passion.

So he would rise for his evening meal and prayer, and when he had completed them he would go to bed, to sink before long into a restful sleep, and to dream of his proud past and his future made splendid by the Mahdi's return. At dawn he would rise to recite the

---

1. A long, white garment worn by the poorer classes in Egypt.

morning prayer and read the Litanies of Sidi Gulshani[2] and the Praises of the Prophet until, with the first warm shafts of sunlight coming through his narrow window, he would rise slowly, put his basket on his back, and turn towards Hilmiya to begin his daily round.

This had been his way since he had come to Cairo fifteen years earlier, and he had changed nothing in the order of his life. Buildings had fallen and others had risen, men had died and children had grown up, but 'Amm Mitwalli knew nothing of Cairo and its outskirts but his accustomed round. He had his resting-places on the way, places where he ate and sat a while. There were two especially where he spent most of his moments of repose. The first was a small mosque, by the door of which he would take his mid-day meal, and when he had finished, he would praise God at length and go into the mosque to pray and sleep. His second halt was before the house of Nur ad-Din Bey in Suyufiya, which he always sought after the sunset prayer. There by the palace gate the door-keepers of the neighboring houses and the servants of Nur ad-Din would gather around him and converse of Islam in its former glory and of how it had fallen on evil times. Thereupon 'Amm Mitwalli would rise with radiant eyes and tell them tales of the Return that is to come, with measured and awe-inspiring accents and a powerful and captivating eloquence that won all their hearts. They would all sit reverent and contented, listening with rapt attention to this great saint, as he spoke of the appearance of the Mahdi and the cleansing of the world of its corruptions and the return of Islam to its former greatness. At that time Nur ad-Din Bey would come out of the door of his house leaning on his expensive walking stick. He would walk towards 'Amm Mitwalli and greet him courteously, bestow his gift upon him, and leave him, emitting a haughty and pompous cough.

Ibrahim Bey, the son of Nur ad-Din Bey, would come too—a merry and playful youth in his sixteenth year. He would approach 'Amm Mitwalli crying:

---

2. Ibrahim al-Gulshani, a famous Persian mystic who died in Cairo in 1533–34 C.E.

"Are you still telling of the battles and adventures of the Mahdi and his army?"

"I tell them and I glory in them. I was in command of a thousand warriors."

Ibrahim Bey would roar with laughter and, affecting a posture of reverence, would button his jacket, straighten his fez and raise his right hand to his head in a military salute. Then he would take a piastre from his pocket and give it to 'Amm Mitwalli, saying:

"Please give me a piastre's worth of melon seeds and peanuts . . . O General!"

One day at noon 'Amm Mitwalli went to the house of Nur ad-Din Bey and sat near the gate, as was his custom. The children began to run to him as usual to buy his wares; the servants thronged to him from all sides. When they had settled down in a circle to listen, 'Amm Mitwalli rose and spoke to them in his accustomed manner. But as they listened enraptured to his enchanting words, Ibrahim Bey appeared, and cried:

"General Mitwalli. . ."

The preacher paused and the people turned their eyes in anger and enquiry towards the merry youngster. Without paying any attention to them, Ibrahim came forward and continued:

"My father wishes to see you. Would you please follow me?"

The gathering deplored this interruption. 'Amm Mitwalli left the circle with his basket on his back and walked calmly towards the door, giving his faithful followers a look of affection and apology. He followed Ibrahim Bey into the garden of the palace, and they walked together for some time along a path, leading to the entrance of the visitors' quarters, where Nur ad-Din Bey was waiting for them on a broad seat. He welcomed 'Amm Mitwalli, and, dismissing his son, bade the old man sit by him on the ground.

A brief silence reigned, during which 'Amm Mitwalli repeated in a low voice his thanks to God and his prayers for the Prophet. Then Nur ad-Din spoke, and informed 'Amm Mitwalli, after a brief introduction, that the venerable lady his mother had heard much of him and of his qualities, and desired to meet him and hear his noble religious tales and his wonderful stories of Islam. 'Amm Mitwalli's heart quivered with joy that his fame had penetrated the outer walls of houses and reached the ears of secluded ladies.

Nur ad-Din Bey rose and walked towards the women's quarters of the house, 'Amm Mitwalli following behind him. They passed through a wide corridor and a huge doorway leading into the garden of the women's quarters. Then they walked up the stairs of a dark terrace, and into a hall so vast that hardly had 'Amm Mitwalli crossed the threshold when he was overcome by its magnificence and his heart was filled with awe and wonderment. Never had he seen—not even in the castle of the Mahdi—so vast and magnificent a chamber.

'Amm Mitwalli was still lost in wonderment when a weak, female voice came to his ears. He turned towards the voice and found the lady of the palace sitting on a large divan not far from him and smoking. He walked towards her until he was near enough to see her clearly. She was a Turkish lady with bent back and wrinkled skin, wearing gold-rimmed spectacles and dark clothes.

'Amm Mitwalli advanced towards her, kissed her thin hand and wished her long life and good fortune. Introductions were completed, and Nur ad-Din Bey left them and went his way. The lady spoke and expressed her joy at his coming and her desire to hear some of his tales. He lowered his eyes and began to gather his tales and traditions in his mind. Then he raised his head and began to tell his story with a fluency and with moving accents that fascinated the lady. When he had finished his story she gave him a present—a sum greater than any he had dreamt of—and overwhelmed him with expressions of admiration that embarrassed and confused him. Then he left, repeating words of gratitude and loyalty to her and to her family. No sooner had he reached the garden than a crowd of maidservants began to cluster round him, seeking blessings from him and stroking his sleeves with their hands. They asked him to sell them something of his wares, and he sat happily on the ground, opened his old basket, and began to sell until he had no more. And so he left and went straight to the mosque, where he prayed with forty prostrations, thanking God for His bounteous gift.

From that day 'Amm Mitwalli went often to the house of Nur ad-Din Bey, where he was welcomed with respect and esteem and showered with favors. His condition changed and he began to bear himself upright, always speaking with a firm voice. He rented a better situated room, with new furniture, and changed his diet from cheese, leeks and radishes to rice and vegetables every day and meat twice a week. He was able to make his turban bigger and longer, to broaden the sleeves of his *gallabiya,* to wrap a cheap cashmere shawl around his shoulders, and to wear bright red slippers and a silk sash with a long fringe. He gradually gave up hawking, freeing himself from his weary round. He enjoyed long and pleasant slumbers, and began to give alms to the poor and became known among them as a sustainer of the needy. He could go to the mosque at his leisure to attend the sermons of preaching and admonition, which he could repeat later to the lady, the mother of Nur ad-Din Bey.

So his fame began to spread in the neighborhood and men began to whisper to one another and to exchange news concerning him, and the image of 'Amm Mitwalli, the hawker of melon seeds and monkey-nuts, the man of poverty and infirmity, faded before that of a great dervish.

A group of his followers were sitting by the door of Nur ad-Din Bey, awaiting his appearance, when one of them said:

"Do you think, my friends, that 'Amm Mitwalli is merely a righteous man, who can speak well and eloquently of Islam?"

Another asked him:

"What do you think he is?"

The man replied in a whisper:

"He is one of the Saints of God, one of the Great Ones of the Faith."

"Who told you?"

"Look into his eyes a while, you will see a strange light shining from them. This is a sign that he is a saint. . . ."

"I had an adventure with him which I fear to tell you, lest you disbelieve me!. . ."

The gathering drew nearer to him, saying:

"Tell us! Tell us!"

"I was walking with him once in Sidi Shawish Street and the time was evening. The street was lit only by two oil lamps, giving a weak, pale light. . . .Suddenly a strong gust of wind put them both out, leaving us in pitch darkness. A sudden fear came over me, and I seized 'Amm Mitwalli's hand and pressed it, and he murmured: 'Fear nothing, we are in God's keeping!'"

While they were listening to his words, another man began to speak:

"Now that I have heard your story it is easier for me to tell you what I know about this righteous saint, with whom we have associated much, though we knew but little of his true character."

The group turned their eyes towards him, and one of them said, with avid interest:

"And what do you know of his character?"

The man spoke with a constrained voice and a tense face:

"He is the Mahdi, the awaited Mahdi!"

They craned their necks forward and whispered to one another: "The Mahdi? . . . The awaited Mahdi? . . ."

The speaker went on in the same tone, his voice trembling with emotion:

"I have seen the sword of Prophecy in his trunk, and when I touched it with my hand I was able to heal my son, my son whom the doctors could not cure, who was on the point of death! . . ."

They vied with one another in questioning the man, and he answered them willingly, with much detail. The clamor grew, and the circle was increased by others who came to ask what was afoot, and to listen to the man who was speaking of the sword of Prophecy and the generosity of the Mahdi, whom God had sent a second time to guide mankind.

At that moment 'Amm Mitwalli appeared from afar. The gathering saw him, and the tumult died away. They hastened to open a path for him between their serried ranks.

'Amm Mitwalli came with his deliberate tread, grave and dignified, giving a calm and sweet smile to those who welcomed him.

The people gathered reverently around him, thronging to him and kissing his fingers and the hems of his sash. The man who had touched the sword of Prophecy stepped forward and said:

"My Master . . . my Lord, savior of my son from death! We know you in spite of your concealment. You are the servant of God whom He has sent to guide mankind; you are the vicar of the Prophet; you are the awaited Mahdi. . . ."

'Amm Mitwalli stared at the man in astonishment, and said:

"What are you saying? Are you raving?"

"You can no longer hide your noble character from us. Yes, you are the Mahdi, the vicar of the Prophet, the bearer of the sword of truth amid men!"

"Be silent! Be silent! For I have not this tremendous honor!"

"Did you not save my son from death?"

"I?"

The man who had told the tale of the dark street slipped forward, and said:

"Did you not light up the street with your resplendent face?"

"I? I?"

The man who had spoken previously said:

"The righteous Abu Bakr[3]—may God be pleased with him—visited me in a dream and revealed your character to me."

'Amm Mitwalli murmured in a low voice and leant on the man standing by him.

"The righteous Abu Bakr revealed my character to you?"

He took refuge in silence a while, staring about him. Then he began to speak, as if to himself:

"My children! The Mahdi is a mighty man, mightier and greater than I. I am but a faithful servant of God. . . ."

He did not sit long with them, but returned home early, sunk in dreams.

'Amm Mitwalli was scarcely awake next morning when he heard a knock on his door. He got up to find out what the matter was, and saw a man with a bandaged head and an emaciated body ap-

---

3. The father-in-law of Muhammad, and the first Caliph in Islam (reg. 632–34 C.E.).

proaching him, clinging to his garments, moaning and supplicating.

"Let me touch the sword of Prophecy from your pure hand."

"The sword of Prophecy?"

"Save me from my sufferings, O my master. Have pity on the wretched who seek you, O mighty vicar of the Prophet!"

'Amm Mitwalli let him into his room, and tended him all day. He recited a section of the Litanies over his head. When evening approached, he put him to bed by his side, with the "sword of Prophecy" under his head.

The next day the sun rose on the sick man, and he declared himself to be full of happiness and energy, in a state of health such as he had never known before. He went up to 'Amm Mitwalli and pounced on his hands, smothering them with kisses. His voice bellowed thanks and prayers.

The days passed, and the dwelling of 'Amm Mitwalli became a place of pilgrimage for men from every part, who came to seek a cure for the ills of their bodies and the whisperings of their souls. 'Amm Mitwalli left home rarely, spending all his time straying amid endless dreams. If he awoke from these dreams, he would take out his sword, place it on his knees, and stare at it in bewilderment.

One day 'Amm Mitwalli saw the noble lady, the mother of Nur ad-Din Bey, come to visit him amid a crowd of his followers. As soon as she saw him she knelt before him reverently, took the skirt of his robe and began to kiss it, saying:

"O mighty vicar of the Prophet! I have come to you, submissive and humble, to seek your grace!. . ."

From that day 'Amm Mitwalli confined himself to his room, never leaving it. Sometimes he received visitors, and sometimes he locked the door of his room and let none come near him. He would sit leaning his back on the wall, with lowered eyelids, and would spend long hours in this manner. Then suddenly he would start out of his reverie, agitated and feverish, draw his sword from the scabbard, and thrust at the air this way and that, leaping around the room and shouting, bidding the devils avaunt . . . until he fell senseless to the floor.

The neighbors heard much of this shouting, and they knew that the righteous saint in his hours of retreat was meditating his mighty mysteries. They gathered around his door with intent ears, with souls full of awe and veneration. 'Amm Mitwalli remained so for a few weeks.

One day he was seen to rush out of his room with disheveled hair and eyes that blazed like burning coals, brandishing his sword right and left. . . . He hurried to the nearby coffee-house and began to strike with the sword at those who were sitting there, shouting, "Away, O rebels, O evildoers" . . . and people gathered around him to stop him.

At last he fell into the hands of the police screaming in a weak voice:

"Praise be to God! I have accomplished my mission. I have completed my holy war."

And his strength failed. . . .

Two Stories by Naguib Mahfouz

Naguib Mahfouz is generally regarded as the foremost Egyptian novelist of the twentieth century. Born in Cairo in 1911, he studied philosophy at the University of Cairo and embarked at an early age on a career as a writer. His first three novels, published in 1939, 1943, and 1944—the so-called "pharaonic novels"—are situated in ancient Egypt. Mahfouz has returned to the theme of ancient Egypt throughout his writing career, usually to contrast a heroic past with the drab realities of present life. In the 1940s and '50s, he concentrated on more realistic social-critical themes. Several of his novels are named for specific places, for instance, *Midaq Alley*, after a street in Cairo, and *Miramar*, after a boarding house in Alexandria. Mahfouz attained the pinnacle of his social-critical writing in his "Trilogy" (*A House in Cairo, Fountain and Tomb*, and *Mirrors*), which brought him world fame. In 1988 he received the Nobel Prize for Literature—the first Arabic author to receive this honor.

The two short stories included here were published in Arabic in 1989, and in English translation by Denys Johnson-Davis in 1991 in the collection of short stories entitled *The Time and the Place*.

The Lawsuit

I found myself suddenly the subject of a lawsuit. My father's widow was demanding maintenance. Awakened from the depths of time, the past with its memories had invaded me. After reading the petition I exclaimed, "When did she go broke? Has she in her turn been robbed?"

"This woman robbed us and deprived us of our legal rights," I said to my lawyer.

I felt a strong desire to see her, not through any temptation to gloat over her but in order to see what effects time had had upon her. Today, like me, she was in her forties. Had her beauty withstood the passage of time? Was it holding out against poverty? If the lawsuit was not genuine, would she have stretched out a demanding hand to one of her enemies? On the other hand, if it was specious, why had she not stretched out her hand before? What a ravishing beauty she had been!

"My father married her," I told the lawyer, "when he was in his middle fifties and she a girl of twenty." A semiliterate, old-fashioned contractor, he did not deal with banks but stored his profits away in a large cupboard in his bedroom. We were happy about this so long as we were a single family. The announcement of the new marriage was like a bomb exploding among us—my mother, my elder brother, and myself, as well as my sisters in their various homes. The top floor was given over to my father, the bride, and the cupboard. We were struck dumb by her youth and beauty. My mother said in a quavering voice choked with weeping, "What a catastrophe! We'll end up without a bean."

My elder brother was illiterate and mentally retarded. He was without work, but considered himself a landowner. He flared up in a rage, declaring, "I'll defend myself to the very death."

Some of our relatives advised us to consult a lawyer, but my father threatened my mother with divorce if we were to entertain any such move. "I'm not gullible or an idiot, and no one's rights will be lost."

I was the one least affected by the disaster, partly because of my youth and partly because I was the only one in the family who wanted to study, hoping to enter the engineering college. Yet even so, I did not miss the significance of the facts—my father's age and that of his beautiful bride, and the fortune under threat. By way of smoothing things over, I would say, "I have confidence in my father."

"If we say nothing," my brother would say, "we'll find the cupboard empty."

I shared his fears but affected outwardly what I did not feel inwardly. All the time I felt that our oasis, which had appeared so tranquil, was being subjected to a wild wind and that on the horizon black clouds were gathering. My mother took refuge in silent anxiety, with each new day giving her warning of a bad outcome. As for my elder brother, he would brave the lion in his lair, pleading with his father. "I am the firstborn, uneducated as you can see, and without means of support, so give me my share."

"Do you want to inherit from me while I'm still alive? It's a disgrace for you to doubt me—no-one's rights will be lost." But my brother would not calm down and would pester my father whenever they met. He would hurl threats at him from behind his back, and my mother would say that she was more worried about my brother than she was about the fortune.

For my part, I wondered whether my father, that capable master of his trade, the man who was such a meticulous accountant despite his illiteracy, would meet defeat at the hands of a pretty girl. Yet, without doubt, he was changing, slipping down little by little each day. He would take himself off to the Turkish baths twice a month, would clip his beard and trim his mustache every week, and would strut about in new clothes. Finally he took to dyeing his hair. Precious gifts embellished the bride's neck, bosom, and arms. Now there was a Chevrolet and a chauffeur waiting in front of our house.

My brother became more and more angry. "Where did he get her from?" he would say to me. Was it so impossible that she might get hold of the key and find her way to opening the cupboard? Would she not take from him something to secure her future? Did she not have the power to make him happy or to turn his life into one of misery and turmoil as she wished?

Arguments would develop between my brother and my father that would go beyond the bounds of propriety. My father would grow angry and spit in my brother's face. In an explosive outburst, my brother seized hold of a table lamp and hurled it at his father, drawing blood. Seeing the blood, my brother was scared, but even so persevered in his attempts to do Father in, with the cook and the chauffeur intervening. My father insisted on informing the police, and my brother was taken off to court and from there to prison, where he died after a year.

"How did she find the courage to bring her case?" I asked the lawyer.

"Necessity has its own rules."

In the midst of our alarm and our mourning for my brother, my mother and I heard the noise of something striking the floor above us. We hurried upstairs and found ourselves standing aghast over my father's body. As is usual in such circumstances, we asked ourselves again and again what could have happened, but no amount of questioning can bring back the dead. It seems that he had had a paralyzing stroke a whole day before his death without our knowing.

We waited till he had been buried and the rites of mourning were over, and then the family gathered together. My sisters, their husbands, and their husbands' parents were there, and the lawyer was present as well. We asked about the key to the cupboard, and the young widow answered quite simply that she knew nothing about it. Sometimes the mind boggles at the sheer brazenness of lying. But what could be done? We then came across the key, and the cupboard finally divulged its secrets, exhibiting to us with profound mockery a bundle of notes that did not exceed five thousand pounds. "Then where is the man's fortune?" everyone called out.

All eyes were fixed on the beautiful widow, who answered defiantly. We had recourse to the police, and there were investigations and searches. As my mother had predicted, we came out of it all "without a bean." The beautiful widow went off to her parents' house, and the curtain was brought down upon her and the inheritance. My mother died. I got a job, married, and achieved a notable success. I became oblivious of the past until the lawsuit brought me back to it.

"It's really the height of irony," I said to the lawyer, "that I should be required to pay maintenance to that woman."

His voice came to me from between the files on his desk. "The old story does on the face of it appear worthy of being put forward, but what's the point of unearthing it when we have no evidence against her?"

"Even if the old story may not be open for discussion, it's a good starting point, whose effect should not be underrated."

"On the contrary, we would be providing the woman's lawyer with the chance to take the offensive and to attract sympathy for her."

"Sympathy?"

"Steady now. Let's think about it a bit objectively. An old man hoards his wealth in a cupboard in his bedroom. He then buys himself a beautiful girl of twenty when he's a man of fifty-five. Such and such happens to his family and such and such to his beautiful wife. Fine, who was to blame?" He was silent for a while, scowling, then continued. "Let's look at it from your side. You're a man who's earning and has a family, and the cost of living is unbearably high, and so on and so forth. . . . Let's content ourselves by settling on a reasonable sum for maintenance."

"Too bad!" I muttered. "She robbed us; then there was the death of my brother and my mother's distress."

"I'm sorry about that, but she's as much a victim as you are. Even the fortune she made off with brought her to disaster. And now here she is begging."

Prompted by casual curiosity, I said, "It's as though you know something about her."

He shook his head with diplomatic vagueness. "A woman who couldn't have children, she was married and divorced several times when she was in her prime. In middle age she fell in love with a student, who, in his turn, robbed her and went off."

He did not divulge the sources of his information, but I surmised the logical progression of events. I experienced a feeling of gratification, which a sense of decency prevented me from showing.

On the day of the court session, I was again seized by a mysterious desire to set eyes on her. I recognized her as she waited in front of the lawyers' room. I knew her by conjecture before actually recognizing her, for the beauty that had made away with our fortune and ruined us had completely vanished. She was fat, excessively and unacceptably so, and the charming freshness had leaked away from her face. What little beauty was left seemed insipid. A veneer of perpetual dejection acted like a screen between her and other people. Without giving the matter any thought, I went up to her, inclined my head in greeting, and said, "I remember you . . . perhaps you remember me?"

At first she gazed at me in surprise, then in confusion. She returned the greeting with a gesture of her covered head. "I'm sorry to cause you trouble," she said, as though apologizing, "but I am forced to do so."

I forgot what I wanted to say. In fact words failed me, and I felt an inner peace. "Don't worry—let the Lord do as He wills." I quietly moved away as I said to myself, "Why not? Even a farce must continue right to the final act."

Half a Day

I proceeded alongside my father, clutching his right hand, running to keep up with the long strides he was taking. All my clothes were new: the black shoes, the green school uniform, and the red tarboosh. My delight in my new clothes, however, was not altogether unmarred, for this was no feast day but the day on which I was to be cast into school for the first time.

My mother stood at the window watching our progress, and I would turn toward her from time to time, as though appealing for help. We walked along a street lined with gardens; on both sides were extensive fields planted with crops, prickly pears, henna trees, and a few date palms.

"Why school?" I challenged my father openly. "I shall never do anything to annoy you."

"I'm not punishing you," he said, laughing. "School's not a punishment. It's the factory that makes useful men out of boys. Don't you want to be like your father and brothers?"

I was not convinced. I did not believe there was really any good to be had in tearing me away from the intimacy of my home and throwing me into this building that stood at the end of the road like some huge, high-walled fortress, exceedingly stern and grim.

When we arrived at the gate we could see the courtyard, vast and crammed full of boys and girls. "Go in by yourself," said my father, "and join them. Put a smile on your face and be a good example to others."

I hesitated and clung to his hand, but he gently pushed me from him. "Be a man," he said. "Today you truly begin life. You will find me waiting for you when it's time to leave."

I took a few steps, then stopped and looked but saw nothing. Then the faces of boys and girls came into view. I did not know a single one of them, and none of them knew me. I felt I was a stranger who had lost his way. But glances of curiosity were directed toward me, and one boy approached and asked, "Who brought you?"

"My father," I whispered.

"My father's dead," he said quite simply.

I did not know what to say. The gate was closed, letting out a pitiable screech. Some of the children burst into tears. The bell rang. A lady came along, followed by a group of men. The men began sorting us into ranks. We were formed into an intricate pattern in the great courtyard surrounded on three sides by high buildings of several floors; from each floor we were overlooked by a long balcony roofed in wood.

"This is your new home," said the woman. "Here too there are mothers and fathers. Here there is everything that is enjoyable and beneficial to knowledge and religion. Dry your tears and face life joyfully."

We submitted to the facts, and this submission brought a sort of contentment. Living beings were drawn to other living beings, and from the first moments my heart made friends with such boys as were to be my friends and fell in love with such girls as I was to be in love with, so that it seemed my misgivings had had no basis. I had never imagined school would have this rich variety. We played all sorts of different games: swings, the vaulting horse, ball games. In the music room we chanted our first songs. We also had our first introduction to language. We saw a globe of the Earth, which revolved and showed the various continents and countries. We started learning the numbers. The story of the Creator of the universe was read to us, we were told of His present world and of His Hereafter, and we heard examples of what He said. We ate delicious food, took a little nap, and woke up to go on with friendship and love, play and learning.

As our path revealed itself to us, however, we did not find it as totally sweet and unclouded as we had presumed. Dust-laden winds and unexpected accidents came about suddenly, so we had to be watchful, at the ready, and very patient. It was not all a matter of playing and fooling around. Rivalries could bring about pain and hatred or give rise to fighting. And while the lady would sometimes smile, she would often scowl and scold. Even more frequently she would resort to physical punishment.

In addition, the time for changing one's mind was over and gone and there was no question of ever returning to the paradise of home. Nothing lay ahead of us but exertion, struggle, and perseverance. Those who were able took advantage of the opportunities for success and happiness that presented themselves amid the worries.

The bell rang announcing the passing of the day and the end of work. The throngs of children rushed toward the gate, which was opened again. I bade farewell to friends and sweethearts and passed through the gate. I peered around but found no trace of my father, who had promised to be there. I stepped aside to wait. When I had waited for a long time without avail, I decided to return home on my own. After I had taken a few steps, a middle-aged man passed by, and I realized at once that I knew him. He came toward me, smiling, and shook me by the hand, saying, "It's a long time since we last met—how are you?"

With a nod of my head, I agreed with him and in turn asked, "And you, how are you?"

"As you can see, not all that good, the Almighty be praised!"

Again he shook me by the hand and went off. I proceeded a few steps, then came to a startled halt. Good Lord! Where was the street lined with gardens? Where had it disappeared to? When did all these vehicles invade it? And when did all these hordes of humanity come to rest upon its surface? How did these hills of refuse come to cover its sides? And where were the fields that bordered it? High buildings had taken over, the street surged with children, and disturbing noises shook the air. At various points stood conjurers showing off their tricks and making snakes appear from baskets. Then there was a band announcing the opening of a circus, with clowns and weight lifters walking in front. A line of trucks carrying central security troops crawled majestically by. The siren of a fire engine shrieked, and it was not clear how the vehicle would cleave its way to reach the blazing fire. A battle raged between a taxi driver and his passenger, while the passenger's wife called out for help and no one answered. Good God! I was in a daze. My head spun. I almost went crazy. How could all this have happened in half a day, between early morning and sunset? I would find the answer at home with my father. But where was my home? I could see only tall buildings and hordes of people. I hastened on to the crossroads between the gardens and Abu Khoda. I had to cross Abu Khoda to reach my house, but the stream of cars would not let up. The fire engine's siren was shrieking at full pitch as it moved at a snail's pace, and I said to myself, "Let the fire take its pleasure in what it consumes." Extremely irritated, I wondered when I would be able to cross. I stood there a long time, until the young lad employed at the ironing shop on the corner came up to me. He stretched out his arm and said gallantly, "Grandpa, let me take you across."